CW01512175

Attendant 14
and the
Factory Girls

Sharon Jeacock

Front cover by Anka Troitsky
https://www.ankatroitsky.com/

ISBN: 978-1-917601-37-5

Chapter 1

Number of admissions: 2717
Admitted: 1845
Age: twenty
Age of first attack: twenty
Married, single, or widowed: single
Religious persuasion: Catholic
Occupation: housemaid
Chargeable to: Oxfordshire
Earlier place of abode: Oxford union workhouse
Nearest known relative: mother
Relatives similarly affected: not known
Children: none but pregnant on admission
Relieving officer: Conway
Insane: two weeks
Dangerous: can be dangerous to others
Name of patient: Esme Barnstable
Facts seen by superintendent: She is quite insane and extremely restless, walks around in an insane manner. She is full of delusions and is adamant that her lover is talking to her through the walls.
Other facts communicated: Mrs Barnstable (Mother) reports that her daughter wanders day and night, looking for her lover, and that Esme insists she is being poisoned by her family, employer, and neighbours. She says she is dangerous to others.

Esme was admitted directly from the Oxford workhouse. Her mother reported at the time of admission that her daughter was experiencing auditory and visual illusions and restlessness.

Esme was quiet and manageable, even being placed to work in the laundry. Her attendant fourteen, May, reported

1

that on July 5th Esme's condition worsened and she was transferred to the chronic woman's block where she continued to rapidly decline.

"And three, two, one. Wake up, May, you are back safe in the room and present day. How was that, May?" Mr James asked soothingly.

I still felt very groggy as I started to come out of my regression. "It was unbelievable, quite something." I could not come to terms with how I had felt and what I had seen. In just this first session, I felt like I had so much more to find out about my past life. I could smell the damp mildew seeping from the thick cold stone walls of the asylum. I could taste the overwhelming dread of what my day would involve, the knots in the pit of my belly urging me to run from this awful place. I could feel my limbs trembling at the thought of what would be expected of me. Being employed as an attendant at the lunatic asylum was not for me, but alas, I had to earn my keep as otherwise it would be off to the workhouse.

"It was all so vivid. It really felt like me."

"Oh, but it was you, May, in every sense of the word. Same time next week? Shall we say 1700 hours?"

I could not wait for my next session. How would I get through the week? It could not come quick enough. But for now, it was back to the present day and the routine that came along with everyday life. Back to the factory. The good old production line beckoned for me for now.

I used to love Saturday mornings. I could lay in past noon, eat brunch, and read the daily paper, take a leisurely walk or watch television. The world was my oyster. I still love Saturdays, but now they are vastly different from when I was young, free, and single. I now have two darling children. I say darling children, but they can be quite a handful at times and at those times I certainly do not describe them as darlings. My bedroom door burst open just as I was having a nice stretch, and two wailing kiddos jumped full pelt on the bed and so onto me. I was not best pleased, I can tell you. Managing to open one eye – the other was yet to play ball – I asked, or rather yelled, "What on earth is the time?"

"It is getting-up time, Mum. Six thirty."

Oh good God, I inwardly groaned. "Let me have another hour," I pleaded a bit too desperately.

"Nope, we want to make you breakfast, Mummy."

"Oh great, lovely," I mustered with about as much enthusiasm as a damp squib. "OK, go and put the google box on and I will be down in a minute."

"Can we put on anything we want, Mum?"

"Yep, anything."

With that my two rugrats were heading downstairs yelling, "We are going to make us all pancakes, Mum."

"Toast and a cuppa will be just fine, thanks," I shouted as the breakfast they had in mind would no doubt end in a cleaning fest for me rather than a treat as I imagined batter mixture flying everywhere. I put my fluffy warm dressing gown on and my oversized slippers and padded downstairs to see what delights awaited me. Toby, eight, and Millie, five, were far too engrossed watching some over-bright, over-loud, over-cheerful cartoon. Nothing wakes you up quicker than that blaring out! Having had my tea and toast, it was back upstairs to try and get myself looking somewhat presentable for the day ahead. Running the water for my wash, I happened to catch a glance of my reflection in the bathroom mirror. *Dear God, when did I get so old and haggard-looking?* I thought as I took in my reflection. I was forty-five but, in that instance, looked easily ninety-five with my sleepy piggy eyes and straggly shoulder-length mousey blonde hair. I decided to scrape my hair back into a bun, which I thought would look very shabby chic when in fact it just looked shabby.

Pull yourself together woman, I told myself. *Get some make-up on and sort your hair out and you shall look and feel like a different woman... hopefully!* Now by this point you might be thinking that I am a single mum as I have not yet mentioned a man in my life. I am married to my hubby Steve and said hubby was still asleep in bed. I did not mind at all though as he was up at the crack of dawn every morning and worked very hard and very long hours, plus it gave me chance to get on with the housework and mountains of laundry that seemed to accumulate during the week – kiddos' uniforms and gym kits, not to mention Steve's work clothes, which were the absolute worst. Steve is a builder, so you can imagine what a task it is to wash brick dust, mud, and other unidentifiable muck out of all his clothes. I worked in the local factory, so my attire was easy, jeans and a T-shirt all covered up with a long white coat and a hair net. It made getting ready in the mornings an absolute breeze, none of this what shall I wear or is my hair a mess? Nope, just bung it all up under the hair net.

It was a lovely bright sunny Sunday morning, that orange warming sun that you get in mid-October. The sun was reflecting off the array of vibrant colours from the trees and shrubs, making even the drabbest tree look alive. There was a little chill in the air, but it was still mild enough to wear a cardigan or light jacket. Sundays were normal in our house, lazy morning breakfast followed by a family walk in our local park. It was within easy walking distance and it did us all good to get some fresh air and exercise. Feeding the ducks was a must, along with ending the visit with a hot chocolate for the walk home. So, all shipshape, we were nearly ready to set off. One more job for me was to put the Sunday joint in the oven. We were traditional and always loved a roast with all the trimmings and a large glass of red wine or two for me and Steve, just perfect. You cannot beat the smell of a roast cooking when you have just been out on an autumn walk.

Off we set to the park, scooters and duck food at the ready. It warmed my heart to see both our children scooting off together full of excitement, as I knew only too well that in the not-so-distant future they would not want to be within a mile of me, let alone be seen going to the park together, so I intended to make the most of these precious years.

We arrived at the park and quickly fed the ducks, played on the swings and slides, and had a walk around, taking in the colours and smells of the season. I had always loved this time of year and felt at peace outside in the autumn air. Soon enough we came across the café, so this meant one of the highlights of our Sundays – yes, hot chocolate time. Toby and Millie could not wait to get going on that thick, rich, creamy delight. The lady smiled as she saw the glee on both of their faces. She put extra cream and sprinkles on, and the cups were almost overflowing. Both had to sit down at the park table and take a couple of slurps off the top so they wouldn't spill any on the way home. They had perfect cream and chocolate moustaches, and I could not help but ruffle their hair and give them each a grin and a squeeze. "Right, come on, you two Herberts, time to go home." They ran along in front of me and Steve carrying the scooters. You could smell the sweet hot chocolate in their trail. Weekends always flew by, and Monday would be here again, back to the grindstone.

Chapter 2

Don't you just love Monday mornings? My rose-tinted glasses had well and truly fallen after our nice weekend. Yes, back to the reality of work, school, and routine.

The alarm sounded at 7am. I hit the snooze button for an extra ten minutes, which was fatal. *Let's get this show on the road*, I thought with as much enthusiasm as I could muster. At least I did not have to worry about doing my hair or sorting out what to wear, so that saved about half an hour. I hurriedly made breakfast, sorted the lunchboxes out and the freshly washed gym kits. Now for the onslaught of waking the kiddos. If I had trudged up the stairs once, I had trudged up there at least ten times. I was starting to panic we would all be late, so I had to unleash the last resort weapon, a cold flannel around both of their faces. That never failed to get them going. When and if I get to those pearly gates, my first question to the big man is going to be "Why is it at weekends my two are up with the larks? Yet school mornings an earthquake would be hard pushed to wake them up."

All fed and watered, we were ready to get going, arriving at the school gates just in time as the school bell rang out. I felt like I was on the gameshow Beat the Buzzer! It always sounded far too loud for my delicate head this time of the morning. I must have looked a right state as I had practically run all the way to school with kids in tow, bookbags swinging and lunchboxes going in all directions. I was hot, sweating, and panting like a rabid dog, face looking like a Belisha beacon, and my messy bun was even messier as every step I took, I could feel more strands of hair escaping and clinging onto my clammy face. Now was not the time to come face to face with Lucinda. I am sure that Lucinda was plain Lucy, but since marrying into wealth, she had decided to crank it up a notch.

"Hi, May. How are you, darling?" Lucinda purred. *Here we go, get ready for the brag fest of what a fabulous weekend she had.*

"Hi, Lucinda. All good, thanks. Cannot stop, on my way to work," I managed through gritted teeth.

"You sure you are fine? You look a bit dishevelled," Lucinda simpered.

"Not at all, Lucinda, I have taken up jogging and the kids and I have just jogged to school," I lied shamelessly, jogging on the spot to try and convince her.

"Jogging, really? Oh, sweetheart, how utterly amazing. Are you in training for a marathon or a charity run?"

Good God no, I thought, I would not be doing this for fun – the running on the spot had almost finished me off. But instead I replied, "No, nothing like that, just trying to get a bit fitter. Now I really must get to work."

"Of course, darling, we must meet for coffee or brunch soon."

I was still trying to regain some decorum and get my breath. "Yes, wonderful," I gasped, still rescuing bits of escaping hair and tucking them behind my ears.

"Got to dash, hun, I have a particularly important meeting," Lucinda gushed. *Of course you do*, I thought to myself. "Do you want a lift to work, May?" she asked as she got out the automatic key fob from her expensive pure wool camel coat, pointing it at the brand-new top-of-the-range Discovery.

"No, thanks, Lucinda, got to keep up with the fitness," I replied, bouncing up and down on the spot, looking more like I needed a pee. Lucinda was walking away towards her car, leaving a trail of Chanel No 5 in her wake. She really was a beautiful woman, lovely sleek long blonde hair, which shone like she had dropped a bottle of argan oil on it. Perfect make-up, vivid red lipstick that showed off her fantastic bright white and even teeth. Dressed in four-inch heels with a beautifully tailored black skirt and matching jacket, white silk blouse, and the look all finished off with the camel coat and designer handbag, and of course the Chanel No 5. Lucinda's children were all just as well turned out, of course. Lucinda has twins, a boy and a girl who were in Toby's year. Abbie and Tristan. Tristan's hair was combed down with gel to within an inch of its life, not a hair out of place. Abbie had the most gorgeous long blonde hair just like her mother's, which was styled into two perfect French plaits. Both wore the official school uniform to boot complete with school logo. I bet they didn't have ham sandwiches, crisps, and an own-brand chocolate bar. Nope, they would more than likely have a Marks and Sparks organic free-range egg and cress on wholemeal bread, fruit loaf, a low-fat sugar-free yoghurt and, of course, oodles of fresh fruit, fine orange juice, and lightly salted lentil crisps. I always tried to do healthy with my two, but the apples and grapes were always left uneaten to the point that by the end of each week, we very nearly had mead and cider where it had started to ferment, so crisps and chocolate it was!

The factory was only a five-minute walk away and by the time I arrived, I had recovered from my over-excursion. The factory had a typical Monday morning feel to it, glum, miserable, and depressive just like its workers. Once we had been in work for a while, that feeling would soon diminish. It would only take one of us cracking a joke or repeating a bit of gossip and it soon felt like we had never been away for the weekend. I worked on the production line and had been at the factory two years. It had only been in the last year that I could truly say I had settled in and made a few friends. I say a year as the first year took up all of my concentration and all my time just trying to grab the packets of biscuits flying at a fair rate of knots down the conveyor belt. No way could I take my eye off of the ball and have a chitchat.

Maggie to my right was just lovely and quite a character, always with a tale or two to tell. Sandra to my left was the chatterbox of our line and an avid tea drinker, always wanting a tea and ciggie break, much to the annoyance of our supervisor, Nancy. Then there was Colin on the very end of our little line. It had taken me four months to know his name, let alone remember it or have a chat. I dared not in those early days. If I had, we would have been dealing with packets upon packets of broken biscuits and no doubt received the sharp end of Nancy's tongue. Those biscuits flew down that conveyor belt and I dared not look anywhere but at custard creams and chocolate bourbons. Over time, as I got more confident, I allowed myself the odd glance and smile at my workmates. Now I had worked here for some time, I could even have a conversation. Not one to brag, but for me this was amazing.

We were soon in full swing in the factory and talk turned to the regular Friday-night outing, which we tried to do every other week. Sandra was beside herself as she had seen that a hypnotist was visiting our town's local social club. She was positively buzzing at the prospect. Us others were not so buzzing at the thought of being up on stage and being made to prance around clucking like a chicken or whizzing around like a plane – no, thank you, not for me. I am more of a bingo girl or quiz night at the pub. Anyone who knew Sandra knew just how persuasive she could be, not necessarily nagging but something akin to it, so before you knew it, you found yourself agreeing to anything. We all ended up agreeing to go on the pretence that if we did not like it, then we would leave.

Friday night arrived all too soon and I was not looking forward to this one bit. I would need a couple of glasses of wine for Sandra's latest mad idea. We met at the social club at seven. The hypnotist was not on until eight, but Sandra was busting a gut to get front-row seats at the nearest table. Maggie, Sandra, and I settled down with a glass of wine. "Colin's late," Sandra said, glancing at her watch. *If Colin's got any sense, he will be running for the hills by now*, I thought.

"Here he is. Come on, Colin, get a drink and sit down." Maggie seemed over the moon that Colin had arrived, maybe because there would be less chance of her being called up on stage. Colin was a lovely young lad, incredibly quiet and unassuming, just as well working with us lot. Sipping on his pint, he looked terrified, the poor chap.

"You don't have to get up on stage if you don't want to," I reassured him.

With that Sandra erupted with a shrill shriek of laughter. "Who are you kidding, May? Like we will have a choice." I glanced over at Colin, and I am sure I saw him trembling.

The compère introduced the hypnotist as Alfonso the extraordinary man of mystery. This all seemed too corny for me. Alfonso soon had the crowed captivated with his one-liners and a couple of reasonable magic tricks. Now it was time for the grand event of the night and Sandra was on the edge of her seat, Colin under his. Alfonso boomed, "Right then, who wants to come up here with me and be transformed to a different person or being?"

Sandra could not get up on that stage quick enough, almost falling and breaking her neck when her foot got tangled in the strap of Maggie's handbag. "Come on, you boring lot," Sandra bellowed to us three. Maggie dutifully followed her friend up on stage with several others from the audience.

"Time for another drink?" I whispered to Colin, and he did not need a second asking.

Standing at the bar waiting to be served, I could not help but glance over to the stage. Alfonso was looking every bit the part of a showman, with his black three-piece suit, white ruffled shirt, and a stripe of glittery ribbon running down the outside seams on either side of his trousers. Getting our drinks and making sure it was safe to return to our table, we were both more relaxed as the show got underway. Alfonso had already done his magic on the keen participants by means of walking behind them muttering, "When I touch the back of your head, you will be under hypnosis and will do and understand everything I ask you to do," followed by, "One, two, three, sleep."

This was going to go one of two ways as I saw it, as neither Sandra nor Maggie were anyone's fool and would be sure to call Alfonso out if they even got a whiff that he was a hoax. So, what happened next was unbelievable and unless I had been there to bear witness to it, I never would have believed it.

Alfonso first asked Sandra to hop around the stage on one leg and she dutifully obliged, having the audience in raptures of laughter. Next was Maggie's turn and her instruction was going to be to dance around the audience and say will you marry me to everyone before dropping to one knee. This I had to see as Maggie was a no-nonsense type of woman and would not be made to take part in any sort of tomfoolery out of choice, but here was Maggie doing just as she was told. The scene was pure bedlam, what with Sandra hopping about, Maggie declaring her love to all and sundry, and all the other victims that had been so eager to get up on stage were by this time being chickens, pigs, elephants, and numerous other things.

Soon enough it was time to bring them all back to reality, with Alfonso giving noticeably clear instructions on how that would happen. "Three, two, one, open your eyes. You are now back in the room," Alfonso boomed, looking absolutely thrilled as the audience cheered and clapped and the volunteers looked around at each other, stunned.

Once Sandra and Maggie had returned to their seats, I still could not believe it was real. "Was you messing about? Or was all that real?" I ventured.

"Oh, it was real all right," they both said in unison. For the rest of the night, that is all the two of them could talk about, and I must admit I was intrigued. *What a fascinating thing the human mind is*, I mused.

Still the topic of conversation come Monday morning, it piqued my interest increasingly more. One thing I knew was I did not want to be hypnotised by the great Alfonso, although it made me think of my own past experiences of déjà vu, which over the years had been extremely strong, in the sense of knowing what view I was going to see around the next corner of a town or country that I had never visited before. During conversations with people, I would experience my stomach flipping over as the feeling was so strong that I had said these words before in the exact same scenario, then just like that the feeling would pass, like snippets of an earlier life.

I decided to do some research of my own to track down a hypnotist that specialised in past life regression. I did not want to go into this blind and end up with a cabaret act such as the likes of Alfonso. No, if I was going to do this, I would be doing it the correct way, making sure this person was registered and on some list of reputable professionals.

It took me a good month or more to track down Mark James, and once I had done my diligent checks, I finally plucked up the courage to telephone him and arranged to meet him for an informal chat. Mark was a lovely guy, extremely easy-going, and not in the least bit pushy, and he understood just how nervous and apprehensive I was about the whole thing. Mark's consulting room was very warm and cosy, set in an old-fashioned house. A small open fire crackled comfortingly on the far side of the room, making the whole place glow. The wall to my right was panelled in dark wood with several pictures hanging from it, mostly of countryside scenes. On the left-hand side of the room was an enormous bookshelf with all manner of titles, far too many to take proper notice of. The walls were painted in a deep red colour, adding to the warmth of the room. A desk was in the other corner with yet more books and papers on it. A wooden floor covered by a rug completed the room. A wonderful smell of wood polish made it smell homely and reminded me of my childhood when my mother would be forever cleaning.

Taking the pressure off me totally, Mark recommended a meeting to explain to me all about the process of regression, how I would always be safe, and he would bring me straight back if I felt the slightest bit of unease. Feeling more confident at Mark's reassurance, I made the decision to explore further. This decision would change and alter my life forever. A gold letter opener was in front of my eyes with the warm orange glow of the embers of the fire dancing and catching glints of gold, putting me in the most comforting relaxed state. I was now ready to be transported to another life I once lived.

Chapter 3

1845

Walking up an immaculate long gravelled drive, I notice the vivid colours of the well-kept gardens. Huge roses are in abundance with bees buzzing eagerly from flower to flower, from yellow to pink and red. The fragrance is heavenly and makes me feel heady and calm. The lawns are mowed in perfect rows, the vibrant green a wonderful contrast against all the flower beds, not a weed in sight. The earth beneath looks like flaked chocolate. Archways of honeysuckle are placed throughout the gardens with little metal benches sat between. As I walk down the driveway a little further, I can see in the distance a huge imposing manor house with turrets on every corner. I am feeling scared and worried and get the sense that I do not want to be here. I am carrying my bag with just the few possessions that I own. I am to be given a uniform to wear upon my arrival. I lift the heavy cast iron door knock and rap it three times against the massive wood-panelled door. A surly woman opens it and beckons me to enter. She knows who I am and why I am here. The first thing to hit me is the dark, drab look of the inside of the hall, like it is dead, drained of colour or soul. As we move further into the house, there is a very grand, very old spiral staircase that I am told leads up to the dormitories.

I am being led into a room and given a uniform which is very basic, a full-length, long-sleeved greyish-white dress that feels scratchy and uncomfortable, like it could be made from tweed or some such material. I am then given a sash bearing the name "Oxfordshire lunatic asylum" and lastly a small white cloth cap to keep my hair neat and out of the way. I am to be an attendant at this God-forbidden place.

Next, I am taken to another small room and the moment I walk in, the damp smell hits me. This place is cold and oppressive. It smells like an old church that has been shut up for years, the coldness catching in my throat, my eyes stinging from the acrid stench of staleness and sorrow. I have a bed with a mattress that is very thin and threadbare, and I can see tufts of straw poking through the stained bed I am to sleep on. A small tallboy stands in the far right corner of my room and to the left is a tiny cupboard. In the middle is a cracked misty mirror, and above the mirror the tiniest window I have ever seen. It is more like a slit than a window and certainly wouldn't let any light in. I turn back again and look at my bed. I have a grey prickly blanket with red trim to keep me warm at night.

I feel the tears welling up in my eyes and a lump in my throat as I think back to just a few months ago and how content and happy I was, a mother, father, and younger brothers at home with me, living in a tiny cosy cottage in the rambling countryside. Life was hard and we never had any money. My father caught our dinner most days with the help of his trusty ferret so Mother could make rabbit pie or stew. She would add a potato to any leftovers and make soup. Father also had a gun and if he could afford the cartridge shells, we would have pheasant, which was a proper treat. There was no work, so we all had to do what we could. For several days at a time, we did not eat at all albeit a stale crust of bread spread with the leftover fat from the cooking pot. One thing we did have was a fire that was kept going. It had to be as it was our only source of heat. My mother, brothers Richard and Robin, and I would go wooding for kindling once or twice a week and stand it near the fire to dry out. I could hear the fire crackling and sparking if the wood was still damp and green. Once it took hold, I could feel the comforting warmth and smell the woodsmoke blowing back into our tiny kitchen. Cast iron pots of water were constantly on the go for washing and a pot of tea or vegetables that we would cook if the weather had been kind and allowed us plenty of potatoes and carrots. Yes, life was extremely hard, but we had each other and lots of love. We enjoyed the simple pleasures of the countryside. We could tell the seasons by nature and my father always new when Mother was to get the washing in off the line as he would tilt his head up in the air, do a few sniffs, and just know it would rain within the hour, and he was never wrong. Mother knew about herbs and all things in nature that you could or could not eat. She always said nature had a cure for everything. In the spring, Richard and I would collect elderflower heads to take home to make a simple elderflower cordial, bottle it up, and it would last us the whole summer. The rosehips we gathered were turned into syrup for colds or ailments during the winter months, blackberries and apples turned into pies, and jam and sloe berries made gin, a real winter warmer and Christmas treat.

Mother became unwell, her cough and fever were getting worse, and after a week she had taken to her bed, which was not like Mother at all. I felt uneasy and sick, a warning feeling in the pit of my stomach. I carefully sat Mother up and tried to feed her with some warming soup I had made. It was dribbling out of her mouth and making her rattling cough worse. I was close to tears now, not knowing what to do or how to help my mother. I feared there was no cure in nature this time. I had to try something; we had no doctor nearby. I heated up some linseed, salt, warm water, and a small amount of glycerine, praying to God it would help to bring some relief to this dreadful illness. It did not work, and Mother was getting worse by the hour. Her body was red, and I could feel the heat radiating off her skin. I sat and prayed by her bed, stroking her damp hair and holding her frail hand, begging her to get well and let me see at least some small improvement. Father came into the bedroom with a small tot of brandy and whiskey to try and ease Mother's cough. That did nothing much apart from splutter out of her mouth as she coughed and gasped as the strong mixture took her breath away. Nothing else for it but to go into the nearest town to fetch a doctor. This would be very costly, and we could not afford it, but I had to do something, if only to ease Mother's discomfort.

As I led Doctor Browne into the tiny bedroom, he explained that payment would be made directly to him at the end of the visit. Suddenly I felt overwhelmed and very embarrassed as I had not told him of our financial difficulties. I cried openly, saying how I could not afford to pay him. "Let's have a look at her and see what the problem is first."

After his assessment, he said, "Your mother is very poorly and has influenza. I will treat her with small doses of strychnine, but I must tell you to prepare yourselves for the worst as this is the start of the big sleep."

I fell on Mother and sobbed. The end of my world was around the corner, waiting to take away part of our family of four. "I see you have a few bottles of sloe gin on the shelf. How about you give me one of those for my payment of service today?"

"Of course," I said. What a kind doctor, for he must have known of our predicament as soon as he stepped into our humble abode.

The very next morning as I took a bowl of warm water in to wash Mother, I knew that she had passed over to the next life. I kissed her gently on her forehead and whispered, "I love you. Safe travels until we meet again."

Father went into a depression at once; the light had gone out of his eyes. The very next week Father had the tell-tale cough and my heart sank. It was to happen all over again in mirror image to how my mother went. Worse still, Richard was coming down with this awful influenza now too, the rattling cough, high fever, dehydration, delirium, then the big sleep. In the space of two weeks, I had lost my entire family, now what was I to do? No way was I going to the workhouse. That is what has brought me here to the pauper's Victorian lunatic asylum.

"I am bringing you back, May, enough for today. I will show you the gold letter opener, which you will see clearly, and you will be fully back to the present day, the year 1995."

My eyes opened and I was back. What had I just experienced? I asked Mark. "Your previous life, May," he tentatively explained.

Chapter 4

1995

Monday morning blues had kicked in well and truly this morning. It was damp, dark, and plain miserable outside, matching my mood perfectly. Toby and Millie were feeling the same as they ambled towards the front door. Their reasons were quite different though; they would rather be at home watching the latest rubbish on the television than learning about the important stuff! "Come on, you two, everyone has to go to school, best days of your life apparently."

My reason for this negative feeling was that I could not stop thinking of my regression session, and Thursday could not come quick enough for me, my next session to another time.

Kids delivered safely to school, I made the short walk into work. Clocking in at the ancient card machine made my nerves jangle. The heavy clunk of the card being stamped by the machine really could wake the dead and did nothing to improve my mood. My mate Sandra was just coming in behind me. "Hiya, Sandra, how's you?"

"I'm all right, thanks, my gal, apart from the hangover from hell."

"Heavy weekend then, Sandra?"

"Could say that. I got absolutely rat-arsed," Sandra replied in her wonderful down-to-earth manner.

I loved Sandra as she was exactly my type of person, a wonderful, genuine soul who did not mince her words and would talk to anyone, whether that be a wealthy tycoon or a down and out. Always the same, that was Sandra. I would not want to get on the wrong side of her though as she was not afraid to tell you your fortune, but if you were her mate, she would defend you indefinitely. *I don't think she would be Lucinda's cup of tea, nor vice versa,* I thought with a smile as Sandra certainly did not suffer fools gladly. Yes, Sandra was my type of person and if she took to you, you knew you would be OK.

"What's up with you then?" Sandra knew me well enough by now to know when I was not quite myself.

"Oh, nothing really, Sandra, just Monday morning blues. And coming face to face with Wonder Woman this morning did not help."

"Who is this Wonder Woman, May?"

"She is all right really. Her name is Lucinda, one of the mums at the school gates. She means well," I said as I could still smell the Chanel No 5 at the very mention of her name. "Oh, and did I mention she is bloody stunning and perfect?"

"Now you listen to me, my girl. Don't you ever let anyone make you feel that way. It's what's in here that matters." Sandra touched her heart with the palm of her hand.

"I know, I know. It's just that Monday morning vibe. Roll on Friday."

"Well, come on then, May, let us get going before that old battleaxe catches us chatting." Sandra was referring to our floor supervisor, Nancy. And my goodness Nancy was a right stickler, a very slim, upright woman in her early sixties, I would imagine, short greying hair that was permed so tight the hairdresser could not get the last of the rollers in, as around her hairline at the back the hair was still poker straight. Nancy wore little round NHS-style glasses that managed to stay strategically perched on her very slim pointed nose.

Nancy would walk around each production line very regally like the queen does when on tour, even had the hands clasped behind her back for an extra hint of authority.

If you happened to catch her eye as she went past your line, she would nod her head at you, her expression deadpan.

True to form we sensed Nancy's arrival as she was just entering the factory, taking off her headscarf and Mackintosh coat. "Right, I am going for a quick ciggie while Madame Nancy gets ready to put her supervisor head on." Sandra was gone in a rush of eagerness to fit her last cigarette in before the bell of doom tolled, signalling the start of our long boring day.

We would have a coffee break at around ten thirty for fifteen minutes, and believe me, good old Nancy made sure that it was just fifteen minutes. The kettle had barely enough time to boil and the tea to brew before Nancy was poking her head around the break room door, curling her finger towards her, beckoning to us to return to our lines. I am sure she would have made an excellent sergeant major in the army. She put the fear of God in me with just one look from those icy blue eyes. Poor Colin would positively quake in her presence. "I am sure that Nancy's bark is worse than her bite," I tried to reassure Colin, but he was not convinced, and I cannot say I blame him.

Maggie suddenly appeared red-faced and flustered. "You're cutting it fine, Maggie. Quick, before mini-Hitler sees you." I was trying to walk at her side to shield her, and we just made it to our line in time.

"I've had enough already, May." Maggie was in tears as she explained that she had the fallout of fallouts with her boyfriend. She always had some drama going on in her life, so this was no surprise to me or Sandra. Colin stayed neutral on all things women-related – he was learning well!

"What's happened then, Maggie?" I half-heartedly asked.

"I think he is cheating on me with that cow from the pub," she spat with venom she was so cross.

"Have you any proof, Maggie?"

"Not yet, but I will have. I just need to bide my time."

"Well, until you have actual evidence, try not to overthink it," I reasoned. To be honest, whilst I had sympathy for Maggie, I did not always have the patience, especially with the thought of my next regression session running through my head constantly.

With the four of us in position at the production line, the familiar whir of the machines started up. "Ready, troops," Sandra bellowed from the start of the line. "Ready," we all answered in unison. I was now third in line between Maggie to my right and Colin to my left. Custard creams, bourbons, and malted milk biscuits came whizzing down the line and it was our job to put the biscuits in the correct box, and woe betide any of us that got it muddled up as Nancy was as sly as a fox and did not miss a trick. Ever. Sandra and Maggie were seasoned experts at this, whilst Colin and I were mere novices. Sandra and Maggie would chat away the whole time, laughing and giggling and putting the world to rights. As for Colin and I, we barely had chance to breathe, let alone chat. The concentration about did me in – talk about stressful, especially with old hawk eye burning her beady eyes over us. I knew it must be lunch time as my belly was grumbling for the boring ham sandwich I had packed. It took me three months to look at the factory clock opposite our workstation, and that was a very quick glance, I can tell you. I imagined if I took my eye off the biscuits for more than a second, all hell would break loose.

The bell rang out, signalling our lunch break finally. The talk in the staff room soon turned to Saturday night and what we all wanted to do for our once-a-month catch-up. Sandra and Maggie were all set for a disco night at the local club house. I could see poor Colin squirming in his seat, trying to disappear into it. "I am not sure I can make it this time, folks. Sorry," I said very meekly.

"What? Why not?" Maggie and Sandra both exclaimed, along with a look that said that I better have a good reason as to why I could not come.

"Well, what with my hypnotist I visit, it takes up a fair whack of my wages and I can't afford to do both," I said with much less confidence than I had hoped. You could feel the tension in the room. It felt like I had either murdered someone or stabbed the two of them in the back.

"Well, I think that's very poor, May, very poor indeed," Sandra said through pursed lips.

Of course Maggie had to chirp in as well, adding, "Good God, May, after we both took you under our wing as well. That is not on. You have gone down in my estimation. I thought you had more loyalty than that." Then with the biggest sigh, they both picked up their ciggies and went out of the room.

"What am I going to do, Colin? I really don't want to cause bad feelings between us all." Colin sat staring as if miles away. "Colin," I repeated.

"I don't want to go myself, but looking at how they reacted so badly with you, what choice do I have?" Poor Colin looked puce. "Not only that, but I am also meant to be meeting a girl I have only just met."

"Ah, Colin, that's lovely news. Good for you."

Soon enough Sandra and Maggie swooped back into the staff room, still looking mad as heck. "Come on, you two, please try and understand. I will come next month, I promise." Of course, I was not getting away that lightly as the blank looks and silent treatment I was receiving spoke volumes. In the end I said, "Look, Colin isn't going either." That did it. Both women swung their heads around like a couple of tawny owls.

"Colin, why not?" and here it started all over again. Colin's face now resembled a beetroot, and he was struck dumb, not surprising with two middle-aged women hovering over him like a pair of fishers' wives.

"Oh, for heaven's sake, you two, leave the lad alone. He is meeting a girl, so the last thing he wants to do is hang out with us oldies."

"So you are coming then, May? What changed your mind?" Sandra grinned.

Maggie, not too far behind, announced, "Colin, you have a bird? Bring her with you. We would all love to meet her, wouldn't we, ladies?"

"Yes," everyone responded. What else could we say? Colin was not impressed with me for letting the cat out of the bag. So that was that then. I had been bamboozled into something that I really didn't want to do, but I learnt very quickly only to upset the two ladies at your peril!

The rest of the afternoon went by in a flurry of excitement from Sandra and Maggie, talking about what they were going to wear on the big night out. "How about we all go down the market on Friday after work to get something sexy to wear?" Sandra could barely get yes out quick enough she was so excited. "Up for that, are you, May?" Maggie turned her head to me expectantly.

"No. Sorry, ladies, I don't work Fridays, remember."

"Oh yes, I'd forgotten," Sandra added calmly.

Phew, I got off lightly there. I thought for a minute that they would demand I come into work just so I could go with them to the market. All this time Colin remained incredibly quiet. I could almost hear his brain ticking over at the thought of telling his new lady friend what lay ahead for the first date.

Hurry up clock, please. I could not wait for the hands to reach three. I finished at three to go and fetch my children from school. I don't think this went down well either as the three of them would have to pick up the speed to cover me, although I was still very slow, so I imagined I wouldn't be missed that much. "See you tomorrow, part-timer," Maggie laughed. It was all in good jest. They knew that I had my two little humans to retrieve from the sausage factory. We all called the school the sausage factory as you went the same and came out the same, no room for anything else. The teachers were run off their feet and did not have the time to help anyone who lagged. It was a lovely school, though, and my two were happy to be there. That's all that mattered to me and Steve.

As I walked the few minutes to the school gates, my mind was wandering to my next session of regression. What would I be doing or feeling this time? I mused. I would not have to wait long to find out.

Chapter 5

1845

I am being led by this brisk woman down a long dark corridor. It smells of damp and decay, the acrid smell stinging the back of my throat. I glance either side of me. To the left are long narrow windows with rusty iron bars. To my right is wooden panelling which is rotten and showing what looks like stone walls beneath. Candles are flickering here and there, casting shadows as we pass. I am with another attendant who I assume is going to train me. I can tell she will not be kind as I can feel an uneasy feeling in my stomach. She is being very brisk with me, telling me to get a move on and calling me "girl". Threatening that if I do not keep up the pace and learn quick, I will be sent to the workhouse. I feel tears in my eyes thinking of my family and how I will never see them again, never feel the warmth of the fire, or smell Mother's suet puddings. Never have the love of my father and the protection of my dear brother. I am frightened. I am trembling and feel sick as if I might vomit. I am all alone now, so I will have to make this attendant position work.

The attendant is now telling me how experienced she is and that I am to do just what she says. I do not know her name and she has not asked for mine. She calls me "girl", and I am to call her "miss". Miss has the biggest mole on her right upper lip with thick hairs protruding from it. I will call her "Hairy Mole" in my head from now on.

Hairy Mole has a huge bunch of keys hanging from her apron. I am being shown a large room which I think is the dining room, as I can smell boiled cabbage or greens. My stomach heaves at the thought. Next, we are in what looks like a dayroom of sorts. A lady is sat in an uncomfortable-looking chair with straps tied around her arms, middle, and legs. This lady has hardly any hair, just long strands here and there. She is trying to rock back and forth, but the restraints are stopping her. She has a yard of dribble coming out of her mouth and is repeating the same things. Mother. Mother. Mother. Why is she doing this? I wonder. Hairy Mole wastes no time in telling me that this lady is a lunatic and cannot under any circumstance be left to wonder freely. She would pull clumps of her own hair out and run amok, attacking the attendants and other patients. Next step for this one is a straitjacket, I am told. As I walk past this lost soul, she glances at me for the briefest of moments and our eyes meet, then again the rocking and mumbling continues. I feel a deep sadness for her.

Next, we pass another lady playing the piano, whacking the keys violently, her head almost banging the keys along with her long spindly fingers. "Never mind her. She is always playing that and making a racket. We have no time for her, too busy with the lunatics."

Next, we pass ladies who are elderly and sat in row upon row of chairs, some wailing, some rocking, some dribbling. And some just look dead. One lady is soaking wet with urine, saying, "I am cold. Please help me. Please somebody help." Hairy Mole shoves her back down in her chair, looms over her frightened face, and tells her that if she keeps on crying, she will give her an ice bath. I later find out that this is a form of shock therapy to bring these poor creatures out of their mania.

We pass many more women, young and old. The younger ones are sat reading, mostly the same page over and over again. Some are holding books upside down and staring blankly at nothing. I ask, "Where are the male patients?"

Hairy Mole snaps at me, "Be quiet, girl. I talk, you listen. You have too much chops about you." I feel so scared and anxious now. This lady is not kind at all.

Next is the bedrooms. Rows upon rows of metal beds lined up in one ward, must be forty beds at least in this one. Straw is poking through the threadbare mattresses with one scratchy blanket allowed per bed, no pillows on some. I am overwhelmed by the stench of stale urine and sweat. The pure decay of the beds and walls is making me feel extremely ill. Hairy Mole explains if the beds are wet, we are to leave them so the bed wetters have a cold, wet bed to endure each night. Her thinking, she tells me, is this will make them use the toilet.

There is a small wash basin in this ward. I wonder how all these women can use just one between them. Too frightened to ask, I do not utter a word. Next on the list is the bathroom, which has two bathtubs in the middle of the sparse, cold room. Suspended above each is a type of cloth hammock. I am told that this will be explained to me another time.

Entering the laundry room, I can see bundles upon bundles of identical clothes piled up high, blouses and skirts, knickers, and vests all in the same greyish-white colour. One size fits all, Hairy Mole is telling me, so should the patients need changing, you can just pick anything. Same for the towels and sheets. Even the soap and flannels are in huge piles. I am thinking the pile must stay permanently well stocked as from what I have seen so far, none of the patients are ever changed out of their grubby clothes.

"Kitchen is next," I am sternly told. The kitchen is well staffed from what I can tell. Women in the asylums wear one size fits all uniforms, with the addition of a white apron with frills around the sides, the little white caps covering their hair, trimmed with the same white frilly edging. If you are thought to be less mad, you can work in the kitchen and laundry under strict supervision of the attendants. All I can smell is over-boiled cabbage and lamb fat. Again this smell is making me feel as if I might faint or be sick. Hairy Mole is not happy with my pallor as she notices me curling up my nose. She barks at me not to be so fussy and if I were that hungry, I would be grateful for anything. "You will eat what you are given, girl, or go hungry. You will not last long then, I can tell you."

I am fighting the urge not to run as a tear threatens to spill over my bottom eyelid. Instead, I reply meekly, "Yes, miss."

Now we are walking down a very dark and gloomy corridor, which has a familiar smell of mildew mixed with stale body odour. I am trying to breathe through my mouth as the stench is stinging my nostrils. Either side of me is thick stone walls seeping water, which is covering some sort of green algae from the years of damp. This is where the mad lunatics live; this is isolation. An ice-cold feeling threatens to slice me in half. I can barely speak or take in what I am being shown and told. Hairy Mole is instructing another pair of attendants to fetch the matron at once as she points to a locked door. It sounds like a wild animal is being tortured on the other side. "Go quickly now, girls. This one needs a short, sharp treatment of shock therapy." The two young girls run off obligingly.

I can see a small letterbox-shaped slit in the cell door, and I am gingerly looking through it. What I am looking at is what nightmares are made of and much worse. A young girl, no more than twenty, is on a concrete bed with a thin mattress, trussed up in what looks like a grey sheet with leather straps encapsulating her. Her hair is wild and matted, hanging in clumps around her frail shoulders. She is wailing, screaming, and thrashing about the bed, as much as she can. Her eyes are wild, red, and swollen. When Hairy Mole says, "Shut it now," this woman spits and swears in our direction. "You have a shock coming your way, my girl," Hairy Mole shoots venomously in this wretch's direction. This is making the woman even more furious, her back arching off the bed, spit flying everywhere, and a garrotted growl is coming from deep within. I think she might be a witch and when I repeat this to Hairy Mole, she laughs hysterically and says, "She is no witch, just mad."

We must always work in pairs, I am told as we wait for the matron and the two attendants to return. I do not need to ask why on this occasion. I am terrified, and I do not feel I can do this job, especially down in the depths of these dungeons. I carefully sneak another look through the viewing window and take in the padded brown leather squares that are in place around this young women's cell. It is soon explained that this is a padded cell, and the pads are to stop the lunatics hurting themselves once they have had the straitjacket removed. So, a straitjacket is what is encasing this woman. I can hear others screaming and shouting in the other cells, shouts and cries of "Let me out, you bitches. I am going to kill you all." Another screams manically, "I will cut out your tongue and dig your eyeballs out and make you eat them." I am told they mean every word and it would happen for sure if they were ever let loose.

I am feeling intrigued now as I take in the noises and the smells. What has made these creatures act this way, or driven them to such madness? I can now hear not far away from where I am standing, another voice screaming, "My baby. What have you done with my baby?"

I ask Hairy Mole what she means, and I am met again with a gruff reply. "Her baby died at birth, and she thinks she can still hear it and see it."

"Poor lady," I just manage to reply before my head is bitten off with, "No good being soft, girl. The woman is a lunatic and suffering delirium and melancholia."

Hairy Mole is getting mad now. I see she is walking up and down the dark corridor, tutting and making a noise as if she is sucking in her bottom lip. She is impatient and thinks Matron is taking too long. This martyr is not used to being kept waiting. Up and down, up and down she walks. I can hear her thick black boots on the stone floor with every step she takes. I can smell her as she glides past me; a stale smell of unwashed skin catches in my throat again. I feel overwhelmed and frightened down here, all alone with this nasty, horrible attendant. At least the lunatics are under lock and key.

Hairy Mole is now walking to the far end of the corridor, glancing in all the other viewing windows, shouting at the patients as she goes along each cell. I take this opportunity to have a quick look in at this wild young woman and just as I am looking into the gap in the top of the door, this woman looks me square in the eye. She is whispering, "Help me. Please help me. You have got to get me out of here." For the briefest of seconds, I have an overwhelming feeling that I must help her. For those few seconds I can see normality in her eyes. I do not know what to do, only that I must help her and try and speak to her alone. I am feeling dizzy now, unsure, unreal. I do not like this feeling that is starting to come over me. My feet feel as if they are on fire, and this feeling is creeping up my entire body. My chest is tight, and I feel as if this wave of heat is going to burst out of the top of my head.

"You are safe now, May. Open your eyes very slowly and when you have opened them, you will be completely safe and back in the present time." I was extremely pleased to hear Mark's familiar voice.

"You are having these feelings as you would have been feeling them back in 1845, completely normal, although it can be very unnerving. I understand at this point if you do not want to explore further. No pressure at all and I will understand totally."

"Same time next week OK with you, Mark?" I smiled as I got up to leave. No way could I stop now, and no way could I leave this woman all alone. I had a strong, all-consuming feeling that this was just the start of things to come.

Chapter 6

1995

"Here she comes, good old May. Come on, gal, be quick and you can have a ciggie before that bloody siren goes off." I could hear Maggie before I saw her, bellowing down the courtyard outside the factory. God, she had a foghorn voice, especially at this time of the morning.

Maggie and Sandra were dragging every bit out of their cigarettes as I sauntered over to them. "Still up for Saturday night, I hope, May?" Sandra asked, sounding more like a threat than a question.

"Yes, all being well," I muttered back.

"Here he comes, love's young dream. Hiya, dreamboat. How is you doing?" Maggie shouted at poor Colin as he was trying and failing to sneak in unnoticed. "Not trying to avoid us are you, Colin?" Of course, this had both Maggie and Sandra in fits of shrieking laughter, barely able to contain themselves. Colin was looking even more sheepish than usual, head down, bright red in the face. It looked like he wanted the ground to open and swallow him whole. I now understood wholeheartedly where that saying must have stemmed from.

As I lit my ciggie and inhaled that first puff, I wondered how this disco night was going to pan out. Sandra and Maggie meant well, but they just didn't know when they were pushing people too far. I could hear the two of them planning what to wear and how darn good they were going to look. I then had a sense that two pairs of eyes were burning into the side of my head. "What?" I asked, dreading the answer.

"We have a little initiation for you, May, something that we know you will enjoy. Or at least we will enjoy." The pair of them grabbed onto each other they were laughing so much.

"What?" I repeated. I had a bad feeling about this.

"We want you to ask old Nancy to come to the disco."

Why would they want her to come? As far as I could tell, they were not her number one fans, and she certainly was not theirs. "Are you mad? Why on earth do you want Nancy to come for? I thought she would be the last person you would want there."

"We want to find out who she really is, as there is more to that one than meets the eye," Maggie mused suspiciously.

"Don't be silly, Maggie, she is just a normal lady doing her job. Leave her alone for heaven's sake."

"Spoil sport," cackled Sandra.

As we stood in our usual spot along the production line, I could hear the familiar clip clop of Nancy's shoes. The Blakey's on her heels must be new as they sounded sharper than normal. "Excuse me, Nancy. Can I have a minute of your time, please?" Maggie was wringing her hands in anticipation. Oh no, I knew what was coming next.

"What is it, Maggie? I am terribly busy. Be quick."

"May would like to ask you something, Nancy."

So, there it was. I had done the dreaded deed, and I had asked Nancy to the disco. Nancy did seem flattered and excited that I had asked her. I just hoped and prayed she did not turn around quick as she would have seen the two giggling Gerties just as excited as Nancy was.

Friday night came around only too quickly for my liking. Time to face the music. I wanted to get there early to bag a table, but of course Maggie and Sandra had beaten me to it. Dressed in their glittery tops and black miniskirts, they certainly looked the part, hair bouffant and hairspray in handbags, ready for the regular bathroom trips to reapply the fire-engine-red lippy and another backcomb of the hair. They looked a right glamorous pair. Before too long we were knocking back the martinis in good nineties style. Suddenly, Maggie said "'Ere they are. Look at the pair of them, like a couple of love birds." I honestly thought I was going to wear her martini.

"Colin, sit next to me. Quick, sit down." I beckoned to the awkward-looking pair.

"This is Bella." Collin introduced his lady friend with equal measures of delight and fear, the familiar redness creeping from his neck up to his face. For once at least the two giggling Gerties were tame. They were far more interested in looking at the entrance for Nancy.

Oh my goodness, Nancy arrived at last and what a most wonderous, remarkable sight she was. Unrecognisable in a sparkling skintight off-the-shoulder red dress, her long greying hair hanging in soft waves below her slender shoulders. Gone were the national-health-style glasses, replaced with contact lenses, I imagined. Make-up done to perfection with blue and dusky pink eye shadow, black mascara showing off her big blueish-grey eyes. The red lipstick accentuated her Cupid's bow perfectly. Tan sheer tights and red high-heeled stilettoes completed the look. "Wow, Nancy. You look stunning," I said, still not believing my eyes. The giggling Gerties had at last stopped giggling and their mouths were agog. Colin was looking the most relaxed I had seen him in days, as all eyes were off him and Bella. I could feel the relief exuding from them both as they drank their lager and held hands.

Pulling up a chair, Nancy sat down in true ladylike fashion, crossing her legs and sitting very slightly to one side, hand resting on the leg. Glass of Asti in hand, she really was picture perfect. "God, you scrub up well, Nancy. I bet you are a right dark horse on the quiet." Maggie got nowhere despite her digging, much to her annoyance.

Next, drinks flowing and music pumping, we all found ourselves on the dance floor, Colin included. Nancy really let herself go and was having the time of her life, dirty dancing with as many men as she could get hold of. Overall, it was a very enjoyable night. We were at the bar as the night was ending, listening to the cheesy slow smoochy dances. Of course, Colin and Bella were making the most of this time together. Young love at its best.

A blaze of red caught my eye, and I nudged both Maggie and Sandra as Nancy the uptight work tyrant was being anything but uptight. One bloke's hands were all over her, and her hands were mirroring his. I could not believe my eyes and nor could the others. It certainly wiped the smile off two faces.

Just goes to show you should never judge a book by its cover, as I would be finding out soon enough.

Chapter 7

1845

I have been here two weeks now and slowly getting into a routine of how the day-to-day running of the asylum works. The asylum days are long, rigorously planned, and highly controlled. We unlock the patients' bedroom doors at 6am. I help to wash the patients that are unable to clean themselves, brush their hair, and examine the condition of their skin. At 9am, following breakfast, we are to take the patients to the "airing courts" and gardens while the wards are being cleaned by some of the attendants and patients. Bedtime is 8pm, and the patients sleep in long rows of beds which are about two feet apart.

I have learnt that there is a male wing in the asylum. All the male patients are looked after by male attendants. They keep the men and women apart, aside from rare occasions like around Christmas time when there is a ball, and patients and staff can dance and later eat Christmas dinner all together. A chance for all to mix. Only the ones considered the most well behaved are allowed to attend this grand event. Another get-together happens twice a year when the staff put on a play for the patients and on occasions the local church helps with this as well, organising the costumes and music. I am told what causes the great excitement is during the summer months. If the weather is clement, the patients can eat a picnic outside in the beautiful grounds. Again this is only granted to the more sensible ones, the ones that will not suddenly scream manically or launch into a frenzied attack on the other patients and staff.

There is about six hundred living within the asylum, including staff. I am answerable to a matron and the superintendents of the asylum, and they are overseen by an alienist, who also has the power and responsibility of the patients in their care.

A farm lays to the west of the asylum, where the male patients are put to work. The more able men enjoy the fresh air and a few hours away from the institution, growing potatoes, carrots, cauliflower, cabbages, beets, and all manner of other edibles. Flowers are also very prevalent, not only on the farm but also in the beautifully manicured grounds. A bit further along from the vegetable plots, there are animals as well. Sheep, pigs, cows, and chickens. The idea is that they want to make the asylum as self-sufficient as possible. Growing all their own crops and getting milk from the cows, meat from the wild stock.

The asylum, along with the farmland, also has a large working kitchen where again the more able and willing women work under the supervision of staff. The smell of freshly baked pies that hits you is wonderful, but it is the fresh bread that is my absolute favourite. It reminds me of home, and I can visualise my dear mother's red face looking at me as she is kneading the dough.

The laundry I have been shown briefly, and from what I can see, there are about fifty women that work there. All the washing is being done by hand, and a huge mangle is always in use. In the far corner of the steamy laundry, there are about twelve women darning socks and mending the bundles of clothes.

The best of the crops are loaded onto a barge by the patients and staff and shipped to London for sale, providing income for the asylum. It explains why we are often served the slops.

The food that is served in the dining room is worlds apart from the food I had seen being prepared earlier. No doubt the more senior staff had all the best pickings first.

The breakfast is usually bread and a very watery gruel along with a cup of milky tea. Dinner is at twelve and is normally lamb stew, which has the look of dirty dish water, and the lamb is a small piece of fatty, grisly mutton all swimming in this thin water. Mashed potato and cabbage are also served with the meal, grey potatoes and watery, slimy cabbage that has been so over-boiled it is white instead of green. This is all followed again by the awful cup of milky lukewarm tea. If time and money allow it, the patients also have the chance of a cup of cocoa, a chunk of bread, and a small morsel of cheese.

I am working alongside another attendant. I was relieved when Hairy Mole informed me. As we had to work in pairs, this other lady was to be my partner. I do not know this attendant's name either. She has a softer face than Hairy Mole. She is as short as she is fat, a little stout woman with three double chins that rest with ease on the neck of her uniform. She has the same hair as most of us, long and tied in a bun, though slightly greying around the sides and temple. I can see it is very thick and wiry all piled under the white frilly cap. Her eyes are sharp. Vivid blue like ice.

We enter the day area where the more able patients are sitting in their chairs, playing the piano or dancing and twirling around. Doing no harm. It is time to take a few at a time into the airing courts. They are allowed about half an hour and then we bring the other patients out. One of the older patients, whose name is Alice, catches the eye of my new partner. She is asking Alice what she is hiding in her pocket. Alice is protesting loudly, saying that she is hiding nothing. A scramble breaks out and a box of matches is promptly retrieved from Alice's pocket. I am told that Alice has a deep obsession with fires and in particular starting them. Fifteen years ago, she set fire to her parents' house, killing them both, as well as her brother and two sisters. After spending fourteen years in a padded cell, she improved enough to be let out of isolation and to be on the main ward. If this continued, she would soon find her way back down the cells. How my partner could tell that Alice was hiding something, I do not know. I do know that she does not miss a thing, so I shall now call her "Beady Eye", but only in my head of course.

The next morning, I wake in plenty of time to begin the long, exhausting day that lies ahead of me. It is early summer, and the mornings are getting lighter, so the dawn chorus makes sure that I am awake. For the briefest of moments, I think I am back at my home, my lovely home in the countryside. I loved this time of the year back home. I would be awake in my bed with the window open, listening to all the birds chirping happily. The sweet heavenly smell of the honeysuckle and sweet briar drifting in through my window. The house slowly coming to life.

What a stark contrast to how this summer has started, the barred dirty windows I cannot see out of, everything looking dull, damp and tired. My room smells like an old church that has been closed for months. My candle has worn down to nothing. The wax, which has spilled over onto the small wooden bedside table, has set as hard as marble. The room is unloved and uncared for. Just like I feel.

I am now being summoned to the matron's office by Beady Eye. I knock on the door like a little scared mouse. Is this my lot? Is this when I am going to be sent to the workhouse?

I am hearing "come in, girl" as I open the door, not prepared to receive my fate. The superintendent, matron, and Hairy Mole are all stood together, looking at me with faces I cannot fathom. I am now being instructed by the superintendent that a female patient is coming onto the ward. She has spent two months in the padded cells for melancholy and madness. They are pleased with this woman's progress, and they are asking me, or rather telling me, that I am to be her personal attendant, along with Beady

Eye and Hairy Mole. I am told that on admission this young woman was considered a wild, mad lunatic. She had accused her family and her neighbours of poisoning her. This woman could hear voices talking to her, telling her of the poisoning that was going to happen. She told people she had a lover whom she was going to run away with and marry. She was thought of as a mad, immoral lunatic.

"We want you to watch her mental state and see if she is safe to be in the main ward. She will need constant watching. Her name is Esme."

"May, you are back with me now. You are safe." The golden letter opener had brought me back from somewhere I was not ready to leave just yet.

Chapter 8

1995

Getting ready for work this drab Monday morning was feeling so much harder than normal, not just because of the dank late November weather. I could not get the asylum and Esme out of my mind and wanted to go back to my earlier life to find out what happened next. I would have to wait for my weekly session as these did not come cheap, and on my factory girl wage I could barely afford the once-weekly sessions as it was. I looked out of my kitchen window, and it was one of those mornings that did nothing to improve my mood. Damp was in the air along with a thick fog, the type that catches any passing smells. Petrol fumes from the cars, busses and lorries lingered all the more on a fogging morning.

I had to talk myself out of this blue mood, buck myself up and get the kiddos ready for the onslaught of Monday morning and all that entailed. It had been a terribly busy weekend in our household, as both of our children had decided to start football. I thought it would do them both good to start some kind of sport. When Steve explained that he had found both a girls' and boys' team looking for fresh players and both practised on a Saturday at the same time, he was beside himself and was far more excited than both Toby and Millie put together. This first burst of excitement was short lived though as I explained to Steve that unless there were two of him or he could divide himself in two, how would he get two kids to two different football training grounds? After a lot of thinking about how we would get Millie to her game across town, Millie then piped up and said that the little girl opposite played in the girls' football team and she was friends with this girl as they were in the same class at school. Her name was Lucy and I remembered the two of them playing together occasionally. So, all was not lost, and Steve got to take Toby, and Lucy's mother kindly took Millie.

The next thought to enter my head was boring, but any busy mum will understand my excitement of having the house all to myself for the entire morning, so what should I do? I pondered. Catch up with the latest shows that I had recorded or do the housework? I knew which I would have preferred. Without a doubt it would have been catching up on *Heartbeat* with a steaming mug of coffee and a couple of chocolate biscuits. Instead, I opted for the sensible mum choice of boring laundry and housework. Well, at least it would save me time in the week as I was always chasing my tail and playing catch-up. Washing machine on, polishing and hoovering downstairs done, all that was left now was the upstairs bath and toilet.

"All finished," I said to myself as I collapsed, content but knackered, onto the sofa. I was looking forward to my children returning home so I could find out all about the football, and I hoped they had enjoyed it. For now, though, I was more than happy to sit in peace and quiet and listen to absolutely nothing. I could just hear the mantel clock ticking comfortingly and the slow, quiet thrum of the washing machine. Bliss.

My peace and quiet did not last long, as before I knew it, I could hear Toby before I could see him. As I peeked out of our front room window, I could see Steve crouching over what looked like a mound of mud. How odd, I thought. This mud pile was now on the move. It started to rapidly dawn on me that this pile of mud was indeed none other than Toby! I ran to the front door faster than Zola Budd. "What the hell, Steve," I cried, still hardly daring to look at the state of Toby.

"He has had a wonderful time, love. Haven't you, lad?" Steve replied, ruffling Toby's hair as he spoke, both grinning up at me like a pair of Cheshire cats.

Forget asking about asking how the football went. All that came out of my mouth was "Stop. Do not come any further."

They both looked at me and in unison said, "What!"

"Your muddy boots! Look at the absolute state of you, Toby." Now when I say muddy boots, I do not just mean a bit of mud; that I could cope with. No, I am talking caked, with big clumps of clay and mud and tufts of grass sprouting out in all directions, shinpads and all. "My God. What happened?" My hands were on each side of my head as I stared in disbelief, taking in half the football pitch that had attached itself to my boy's face, arms and legs.

"I played footie, Mum, and loved it."

"I can see that, son. Did you leave any of the grass and pitch behind?" I added, only half joking.

"This is how it will be from now on, May," Steve pitched in, adding, "He loved it and really got stuck in."

"So it seems," I half-heartedly replied. I was already processing my next move. "Right. Do not move. Take everything off in the porch," I instructed, already imagining the mess this was going to make. I am by no means house proud, but when I had just spent all morning cleaning, you can understand my over-reaction. My own fault, I know, and one I shall not be repeating. Once Toby had deposited his muddy clothes into the bin liner I had flung at him, I reminded him to have a nice warm shower. "Not a bath. A shower," I ordered as I could just imagine the state the tub would be in after a bath. "And make sure you swill the shower down after," I added as an afterthought.

"I will, Mum. I promise."

After making a cuppa, I had just sat down when I heard, "Hi, Mum. I am home." Millie was about to step in the door.

"Stop," I repeated, being more prepared this time around. Millie was not in half as bad a state as her brother.

"You know, May, they both really had a great day today," Steve said as he sat down next to me that evening.

"I know they did, Steve," I replied, squeezing his hand lovingly. I was just so grateful that I had such a wonderful, caring husband and a great father for our children. On a side note, though, I did add, "Wouldn't Toby be more suited to badminton and Millie to ballet maybe?" We both looked at each other and shared a laugh.

So, to say I was not in the mood for work was not a lie and I could well do without Maggie and Sandra going on in my ear. I just wanted to do research today on the old Victorian lunatic asylums, either this one in Oxford or any others in the country. I needed to get a feel for how this poor young woman felt. I was becoming all consumed with my other life. I could not wait to find out more later in the week. But for now, work it was.

Kiddos dropped off at school, I began the familiar walk to work. As I approached the tall black iron gates, I saw blooms of smoke curling slowly in the still foggy air. Of course, it was Maggie and Sandra having the first of many cigarettes of our working day.

"Watch you, May," they both bellowed across the yard.

"Morning, ladies," I replied, sounding much more cheerful than I felt. I could see Colin had already arrived as his bike was in the bike rack. "Is Nancy in yet?" I enquired as I lit up my ciggie.

"Course Nancy is in. She probably sleeps here. I wouldn't be surprised." Maggie laughed.

I was still thinking of our night out and how glamourous Nancy had looked. She had acted like a different person. I had a niggling feeling about Nancy, something strange that I could not put my finger on.

The biscuits were flying down the conveyor belt at top speed this morning. Or was it because I was still feeling a bit down? Maggie and Sandra were gossiping away as usual. Colin was Colin and seemed to drift off to his dream world even more than normal. Probably daydreaming about his new girlfriend.

Talk soon turned to Christmas and all the excitement that the festivities brought in and outside of the factory. It was only late November, but it gave us all something different to talk about and made the day pass that little bit quicker. I then heard the dreaded words of "The Christmas do!" and I groaned inwardly. Maggie and Sandra were eagerly telling Colin and me all about what we could expect from the night, explaining in detail what would be expected of us. The boss, Mr Tooley, hired a local hotel along with a disco, and there would be a wonderful three-course Christmas dinner with all the trimmings, red and white wine aplenty on all the tables, and jugs of water. Money would be put behind the bar for us to have a couple of drinks if we wished. Once the money pot was gone, it was then down to us to buy our own drinks. "Very generous of Mr Tooley," I replied to both.

"Well, he can afford it, and we get bugger all else out of him for the rest of the year." Goodness, Maggie could be so cynical at times.

Sandra chipped in. "Too right, we work like slaves, us lot. We make the most of him at the Christmas do."

Considering around fifty staff worked for Mr Tooley, this Christmas outing would not be cheap. It was decent of him, I thought, not daring to say it aloud.

"Can partners come along?" Colin pipped up. This was met with loud, unrestrained laughter.

"No way," they both echoed. "What and spoil our fun?" they said as an afterthought.

This was a few weeks away yet, giving me plenty of time to come down with one lurgy or another. I really did not fancy it. I got so tired after working and looking after my family that when I got home, I just wanted to cosy up on the sofa and watch my soap operas. Once upon a time I was a party animal and out until dawn, still up to go to work for my 7am shift at the local corner shop. Those days were well and truly over, but of course I nodded my head in enthusiasm to my two workmates, saying that I could not wait and how it sounded like it would be a fantastic night. I slyly looked across at Colin and the look on his face told me all I needed to know.

But for now, I had more important things to occupy my mind. As that Monday workday ended, I stepped outside. The fog hadn't lifted all day, and the air was thick with smog and pollution from all the local factories. The light was fading as I walked to collect Millie and Toby from school, the sky a dismal grey. The few leaves still clinging onto the trees were drooping and sad-looking. In the distance I could hear a pigeon cooing hauntingly. Something felt dark and ominous about today, as if someone was trying to tell me something. I had an overwhelming instinct of what that might be, but I would find out before long. I just knew it.

Chapter 9

1845

I am awake in my bed, full of trepidation of what this day will bring. This is my first day of being the attendant to Esme. I am feeling nervous, scared, and sick. I need to get washed and dressed in my uniform and report for breakfast. Then I am to wash and dress the patients as usual before overseeing their breakfast. All my chores still have to be done before I am to go and meet Esme. I pull the stiff, itchy woollen blanket off me and place both feet onto the ice-cold stone floor. It is a freezing winter morning, so cold that ice has formed on the inside of the window, and I can see my breath in the air. I have no hot water to wash in, so for this I go a short way down our corridor where there is a small kitchenette off to the left. This is for the staff on my landing. The range is still alight, and I put a pan of water on top. It's kicking out some heat, so I don't have to wait long until my pan of water is steaming and I am carrying it back down the corridor to my room. I am shivering and have goosebumps all over my body, so I tense all my muscles to try and protect myself from the bitter cold. I empty the now barely warm water into the chipped ceramic bowl, then wash as quick as I can. A lick and a promise is what my mother would refer to it as. Pulling on my grey dress, apron, sash, and finally my frilly cap, I am ready to face whatever the day has in store for me.

The watery gruel sticks in my throat this morning; I feel I might choke. I am forcing it down as best I can, as I know it will be hours before I eat anything else. My eyes are watering, and saliva is building up in my mouth. I grab and claw at my throat as if to help the slop on its way down to my belly. I manage half of the gruel. My cup of warm milky tea I manage to get down without too much distress, closing my eyes tight in concentration to gulp the last dregs. My eyes are still shut tight when I feel a blast of stale air rush past me. It is Hairy Mole, and by the smell of her, she has not had a lick and a promise this morning. I doubt her body has seen a cloth in days.

"Ready, girl? No time for sipping tea. We got lunatics to get ready," she barks at me. I stand up to attention so quickly to try and appease her that my chair makes an ear-piercing sound as it scrapes the uneven stone floor. Hairy Mole does not say a word, although her stern look speaks volumes. I could see her shudder at the noise.

I am now in one of the large female dormitories. I can see twenty beds on each side of the room, so forty patients that need our care. How are we going to get all these patients washed and groomed in time for breakfast? As if reading my mind, Hairy Mole growls at me, "Stop gawping, girl. No good standing there with your mouth agog. Get on with the work you are paid to do. Move it." I feel a wave go over my body. It is fear.

I am now looking at an elderly patient sat on the edge of her bed, fiddling with the hem of her off-white nightdress. I approach her and ask if she is well. "I wetted me bed, miss." Her feeble response makes me warm to her. I tell her not to be worried as I can help to wash and clean her and make sure that she has a dry bed to get into tonight.

Her reply to this basic offer is "You not going to cuff me round me head or shout at me, miss?"

I tell her I will not be doing either.

"Ta, miss, I dint mean to do it. Me bladder ain't as good as it were, you see." I can tell that this lady is local because of her Oxfordshire twang. "That tother one always 'its me round me 'ed."

"I shall not be doing that to you," I reassure her.

By this time Beady Eye has joined us too, and never one to miss a trick, she comes charging over. She is cross with me and shouting that I am to get a move on and that we have not got all day. Feeling slightly brave, I explain that this old lady needs my help to get out of her wet nightdress. By now the elderly lady is standing up and I can see that the back and sides of the nightdress are clinging to her, turning the material transparent and showing her white skinny legs. The smell of ammonia hits me at once. This is not going down at all well with Beady Eye, as she is ordering me to just get on with the job in hand, adding, "Good God, girl, if we washed and dressed everyone who was a bed wetter, it would be time to put them back to bed again. Now stop mollycoddling and do your job or I shall be reporting you to the matron."

So that is that then. Hairy Mole is telling me to just wash the essentials, being the face, under the armpits, their rear end, and their fanny Annie. The other attendants expect me to wash and dress the patients along with combing their hair, plus checking the general condition of their skin, all in five minutes. I take this old frail lady by the hand and gently lead her to the sink. The lady is telling me her name is Gertie as she follows my lead without complaint. Gertie is very childlike, swinging my hand in hers. I fill the sink with warm water that I have fetched from a large copper barrel. Taking Gertie's nightdress off, I can see how tiny this lady is. As I gently wash Gertie's back, I can feel the sharp bones of her shoulders beneath the wet cloth. I can see all the bones going down her back. As I wash lower down, I see how prominent both of her hip bones are, how red and sore they look from laying on them throughout the night. I help Gertie turn around to face me so I can wash her front. I can see every rib threatening to burst through her thin, fragile skin. Gertie has the most beautiful snow-white hair, which hangs just below her thin shoulders. I am now dressing Gertie, who is still very compliant, letting me do as I wish.

I brush Gertie's hair and put it up in a topknot for her. As I stand back and look at Gertie, I can see her collar bones rising and falling as she breathes, and two hollow indentations are obvious just above this area. Gertie's skin is in remarkably good condition, apart from the bony areas near her hips. I do not know what treatment is to be applied if we find skin tears or urine burns. I have not been trained in this and feel out of my depth.

I am leading Gertie back to the large ward, and when I enter, what greets me is total mayhem. A young girl, no more than sixteen, is screaming hysterically, running around the ward, clawing at her hair and hugging her shoulders, yelling manically that she is dying. Both Beady Eye and Hairy Mole are trying to grab hold of this out-of-control patient. The other patients are becoming unsettled. Some are rocking back and forth, still in their nightwear, some are mumbling, "Leave me alone. Leave me alone," and others are doing both. Two patients are laughing madly, running amok, reminding me of two witches, their wild hair flowing amid their frenzied laughter. I am feeling frightened. Hairy Mole manages to grab the young girl and wrestle her to the floor. Hairy Mole is now ordering Beady Eye to get the rags and two buckets.

I cannot bear it any longer and finally ask what is happening to this poor young girl. As I look down at them both still on the floor, I can see that Hairy Mole is bright red in the face, her cap is all but off her head, and strands of her hair are escaping her bun. She is sucking her top lip in, hairs and all, desperately trying to hold the girl. I am being instructed to sit on her legs as Hairy Mole is struggling and losing her grip, beads of sweat now running down her chubby face and threatening to drip off her nose and chin.

It is her curse; that's what's up with her. Her curse has arrived, and she has never had one before, I am being told. Trying now to calm this frightened young girl, I say to her that all will be well, this is perfectly normal, that she should not be frightened.

The young girl relaxes slightly, and we manage to sit her on the edge of her bed. Beady Eye has returned with two buckets, one filled with rags. Beady Eye then tells this girl that she needs to clean herself and put this rag in her knickers, change it often and put the dirty ones in the empty bin. "At the end of the day, your last job is to take the dirty rags in the bin and boil them clean," she says. "Always keep both buckets under your bed."

There is no discussion about what is happening to her body, no reassurance or kindly words. Nothing.

By this time, we have calmed the rest of the ladies down and are now leading them into the dining room for breakfast. Matron is already waiting for us, looking at her fob watch to let us know we are running late. Gertie is sitting looking at her gruel but not trying to eat anything. I am going over to her now and telling her to try and eat something. Gertie looks up, her kind blue eyes smiling at me as she shakes her head. I give her the spoon and she scoops up some of the gruel. Her tiny hands are shaking, and the gruel lands in her lap. Gertie tries once more, and the same thing happens again. I am helping her now, guiding the spoon to her lips. Her mouth opens obligingly like a little baby bird. I get three spoonfuls into Gertie before I feel Beady Eye glaring at me from across the room, heading my way. I thought she would be pleased with me helping Gertie to eat something, but instead she is scolding, saying I am not to do it again as it makes the women lazy. Gertie is not lazy, just a frail old lady. Tears are pricking at my eyes now and I feel as though I want to leave this place. I cannot, though, as my only choice is the workhouse. I miss my family and my mother's tender love, remembering how when I had my first curse, Mother had prepared me so I would not be frightened. I look across at the young girl and the stark contrast of our lives. I wonder why her mother never told her about a woman's curse. The young girl is staring at nothing, slowly rocking back and forth. Traumatised.

Once breakfast is over, I am being told to take the patients to the large dayroom. They all follow me like sheep. I sit some of the ladies down in the chairs, most of which are in a semi-circle. Three of the patients cannot sit still, some still rocking back and forth, some wandering about the room aimlessly as if searching for something. One lady heads towards the piano in the far right of the room and begins hitting the keys in no order. This noise at once aggravates another woman, who, to my horror, launches herself at the piano and slams the lid shut, narrowly missing the fingers of the player. The now hysterical woman is screaming, with hands either side of her head, repeatedly saying, "Shut up. Shut up."

Before I have a chance to see the outcome, I am being summoned to the superintendent's office. The matron is standing in the dayroom, beckoning me with her long finger. Matron orders Hairy Mole and Beady Eye to sort out this commotion this minute.

I am now being led in total silence along another unfamiliar corridor. It is very dark with only the glow of the oil lamps lighting a dim path. I am looking at both sides of the wall, upon which sepia photos have been hung of all the staff and patients that have been housed and worked here over the years. I notice that this part of the asylum is dryer and does not have the noticeable smell of damp. Further along we walk until we reach a huge wood-panelled door. The matron raps three times, and a voice says "Enter."

Matron enters first and I follow close behind, keeping my head down, looking at my shoes. The superintendent is now telling me to take a seat. The chair is very upright and made of wood with a red velvet material. The seat is padded, and the wooden arms of the chair have carvings etched into them. I can feel it is old and has been sat in many times. I can tell this as my hands trace over the smooth wood. In some places the pattern is almost worn away. How many have sat in this chair? I am now thinking, still too scared to look up at this important man. As if reading my mind, he orders for me to look at him. I slowly lift my head, and our eyes meet across the oak table.

I am taking in his appearance now. He looks about sixty years old, with a small, kind-looking face. He has greying salt and pepper hair and long, wiry grey sideburns. His long hair is swept back from his small face, tucked in the collar of his white shirt. He is wearing a black suit which shows the whiteness of his shirt. He is not wearing a tie but more of a black scarf around his neck, and I can see it is fashioned into a neat bow. He is now addressing me by calling me "attendant fourteen". I do not respond as my nerves have left me speechless. I do not know how I should answer this man. He is smiling kindly at me, his eyes creasing at the corners behind his little gold-rimmed glasses. "Would you care for a cup of tea?" he asks me, trying to put me at ease.

I have always been told by my mother that it is considered rude if you do not accept the offer of a drink, so I nod my agreement, very softly replying, "Yes, please."

With that the superintendent is using the flat of his hand to press down on a ringing brass bell that is positioned on his side of the desk. Another lady appears almost immediately. I cannot tell if she is an attendant or not as she is dressed differently to me, in a deep blue dress and a little hat. "Please lay a tray of tea up for three." The lady nods obediently but says nothing.

As we wait for our tea, the man behind the desks introduces himself as Doctor Jones. He asks me if I am indeed attendant fourteen, to which I have to say that I do not know, as I have only ever been known as miss or girl since my arrival. I tell him my name at birth was Mable Sullivan but that my family always fondly called me May.

He is inhaling deeply, and his eyes are squinting as if he is deep in thought.

"Well then, we shall call you attendant fourteen along with Miss May." I smile shyly in reply. Doctor Jones is now shuffling paper around on his desk, so many files are laying all around him. An open wooden box catches my eye and I discreetly have a quick look. It is full to the brim of long, fat cigars. To the right-hand side of this wooden box is a decanter of what looks like brandy. The decanter is ice-clear and almost sparkling in the light of the winter sun shining through the clean widow just behind the doctor's desk. I can see the glass is creating a prism effect on all of the papers in front of him. Blues, violets, yellows and a hew of purple make a spectrum of bright colours in this otherwise dull room. Shelves filled with books line many of the walls, some so full I can see them bowing with the weight. A small fire glows in the corner, ambers, oranges and reds only bringing warmth to a small area. The rhythmic ticking of a grandfather clock offers me comfort and calms my nerves.

Suddenly a knock on the door makes me jump. It is the lady coming back in with the tea tray. A patterned silver tray carrying three cups and saucers, milk, sugar, and a plate of jam tarts. I can tell that the jam tarts have not long been made, as I can smell the aroma of fresh pastry. Matron is pouring the tea into the pretty fine bone China cups. The cups are cream in colour with tiny little pink and gold embossed flowers. Matron is passing me my tea, and I thank her as I take the cup and saucer. My hands are shaking, causing the cup to rattle against the saucer, and my tea is spilling over the top. Doctor Jones leans over his desk and takes the cup from my still trembling hand. As he does so I can see his face more clearly as our eyes meet. His little round gold glasses have slipped down his sharp pointed nose, his greying, wiry eyebrows are long and just touching the top of his glasses. As he takes my cup, I notice just how fine the China is, as the light from the window makes the tea show through. I have never drunk from such a pretty and delicate cup.

"Right then, Miss May. Time to get you to work." Doctor Jones is standing up now and opening the door, beckoning me out before him, closely followed by Matron. Doctor Jones is telling me about this young girl as we make our way to finally meet her.

Her name is Esme Barnstable, and she is twenty years old. Her mother became concerned about her erratic behaviour some months ago. Esme was showing signs of mania and melancholia. At night Esme would become restless and wandered the house, talking to the walls, telling them that she was being poisoned and people were telling her she was a liar and an immoral fallen woman. Shortly after these prolonged episodes, Esme would take to the nearby streets where she lived and knock on her neighbours' doors, hysterically accusing them of the same thing. Her mother could not cope with her any longer, so Esme was sent by her family to the workhouse. This was not the correct place for this young girl as she was very troubled and would manically bite, spit, and hit anyone who looked at her. Once she came into our asylum, it soon became clear that Esme was a danger to herself, the staff, and other patients.

Doctor Jones is now explaining that shortly after this young female was admitted, it was decided quickly that she had to go into the padded cell ward of the hospital, where only the maddest lunatics were kept under lock and key, and often in a strait shirt or jacket. After two days Esme's condition deteriorated further. She had stopped eating and drinking. Esme was warned if she did not start eating again within a reasonable time, there would be no alternative but to tube feed her. After another few days, this treatment was conducted. "We also thought it would be right to use cold-water shock therapy along with the purging therapy." The doctor is smiling at me now and telling me how thrilled he was to hear reports from the attendants that this treatment had been successful and all but cured Esme of her insanity. He felt Esme had improved so much that the young woman could have a trial period on the ward, mixing and eating with the other patients, and my job was to watch her constantly and report my findings to him and Matron.

Now I am standing outside of a room, the doctor gently tapping on the door. "Can I come in, Esme? I have a young attendant I would like you to meet. She will be looking after you from now on." No reply comes from the other side of the door. I am told to go in and meet my new patient. With great trepidation I slowly open the door that leads into this tiny stuffy room. I look at Esme and give her a smile. I get no response at all, just a blank deadpan look. But something in those eyes is trying desperately to communicate with me. It is the same look that Esme gave me all those weeks ago when I looked through the viewing window. What is it, Esme? I am wanting to say, but I must be cautious and abide by the rules. For now, anyway.

Chapter 10

1995

Colin was off sick today. Great, that was all I needed. Nancy could not wait to be the bearer of this news and took real pleasure in letting us three know that it would be all hands on deck today, no time for silly giggling and gossiping, adding, "I doubt you will get time for a break, let alone a cigarette."

This did not go down at all well with either Maggie or Sandra, who mumbled back, "We will see about that," then started quoting the latest working rules and how it was illegal to work more than four hours without a break. This cut no ice with Nancy whatsoever, as she replied briskly how they had better get a move on then. I am sure I noticed a very slight smile threatening the corners of her mouth as she walked away.

"Bloody Colin, I bet it is only a sniffle. He wants to man up." Sandra was not happy. Not happy at all.

Maggie chipped in. "Men! Good job they don't have to give birth. It would be the end of the human population for sure." I kept quiet as usual, just nodding and smiling in all the right places. *I bet poor old Colin's ears are burning*, I thought to myself, laughing inwardly.

The morning passed in a blur of custard creams and chocolate bourbons and not much else. Needless to say, Maggie and Sandra were gasping for a ciggie come 10am. Nancy was hovering like a hawk ten minutes before the tea break, making sure we had worked hard enough to allow us fifteen minutes of freedom. Her thin white hands were scurrying in the cardboard boxes that lay at the side of us, checking that they were suitably full of biscuits. She looked almost disappointed when she saw that indeed they were bulging full. It was surprising how quick we all worked that morning with the threat of our ciggie break being taken from us. The ultimate dangled carrot.

At 10am on the dot, the three of us were off like whippets out of a trap. "Maggie, you get that kettle on. May, you get the cups out the cupboard. And I will fetch our coats." Sandra was almost tripping over her own feet as she went.

"Come on. This kettle is on a go slow, just when we are in a blasted hurry," Maggie said, sounding as cross as she looked. I was stood just behind her, empty mugs in hand. I could not help but smile as I saw Maggie hopping and jigging about, first on one leg and then on the other one, as if willing the kettle to boil faster.

We went outside, where the air was dry and bitter cold today and it would not have bothered me if I had a ciggie or not. As the other two dragged long and hard on their cigarettes, it did not take them long to start on about the impending Christmas do, particularly the Secret Santa. As much as I was dreading the Christmas party, I dreaded the Secret Santa even more. I could never understand the point of it. Not spending over a certain amount of money on one present so we would all spend the same amount seemed ridiculous to me. My thinking was why not just buy the person a nice bottle of wine or box of chocolates, or better still just put the five pounds in a kitty for the bar drinks instead of wasting it on some silly plastic apron with a naked man or women on the front... or worse! Of course, I did not dare voice my opinion to Sandra and Maggie. They would be sure to call me a tight miserable sod. I wondered what I would buy Nancy if I were to pull her name out of the hat.

After finishing our second cigarette, we made our way slowly back into the factory, and of course Nancy was just inside the door, making a point of looking at her watch and peering over her glasses at the three of us.

"You three had better buckle down and get on with your work as Mr Bonner is going to be paying us a visit sometime later." Nancy was thrilled at this prospect. I was sure that Nancy had a bit of a crush on old Mr Bonner due to the red hue that spread from her neck up into her cheeks.

Never one to miss anything, Maggie piped up. "Whoa, Nancy, what you gone all red for? Do you fancy him or something?"

Of course, as per usual, Sandra snorted aloud, nearly choking on the piece of chewing gum in her mouth.

"Don't be so stupid, Maggie, of course I don't." Nancy tutted as she pranced off.

"Ah well, it got rid of her, didn't it? She got too up herself lately, that one." Maggie was still smirking as Nancy scurried off.

I had only met Mr Bonner a handful of times, and why Nancy referred to him as "visiting" I do not know. She made it sound as though he was jetting in from goodness knows where on a royal visit when in fact Mr Bonner was only upstairs in this very factory. Admittedly he did not come in every day and when he did come into work, we seldom set eyes on him, as he confined himself to his office. On the few times I had met him, he always seemed a decent sort of chap, tall and slim with jet-black hair, which we all knew he coloured, as Mr Bonner was easily pushing seventy-five if not older. Every day he dressed smartly in grey trousers, gingham shirt and a pale blue V-neck jumper.

Panic stations set in at about two thirty that Monday afternoon. Nancy was running around like a mad thing. Three of the four conveyor belts had packed up and no engineer could come out at such short notice until the following morning. We were all keeping our fingers crossed that we would be sent home early. Dear Nancy had other ideas though and proudly announced in an authoritative voice that "Due to Mr Bonner's impending visit and seeing as the machines have broken, I would like you all to make the most of this time and do some deep cleaning of the said machines."

This did not go down well, not only with myself, Maggie, and Sandra but with the whole work force, and I could hear numerous tuts, sighs, and shouts of "We are not cleaners. No way are we doing that."

"You will do as I darn well tell you if you still want a job at the end of the day." Feeling the pressure of Mr Bonner's visit, I could tell that Nancy was serious, her face taking on a very stern, sharp look. It made my stomach flip. I had seen that look before. But where? I just could not pinpoint it. Was it at the school drop-off or pick-up? She may have been picking up a grandchild.

"I have to go soon, Nancy, to pick up my children," I said nervously as quietly as possible so Maggie and Sandra did not hear, as I just knew that they would not be pleased with me leaving them to clean all the machines.

"Yes. Yes. I know you do, May. Before you go, could you go up to the top floor, please, and fetch a few cleaning products?"

I had never ventured upstairs before. There were six floors to this ancient factory, so I decided to get the service lift to the top floor. This lift looked as old as the factory and was very temperamental. Pressing the call button, I heard the lift juddering into life. It was a slow, old thing and seemed to take an age to reach the ground floor. Opening the main door to the lift, I then had to slide over the internal door, which was a brown concertina plastic door that you had to fold back onto itself. Once inside you had to make sure that you had closed the internal door correctly or the lift would not work, so having done this, I heard the loud bang of the outer door slam shut, and I was going up to the top floor. It really was a rickety ride. Encased in this one-person lift, it felt eerie, as if I were the only person left in the factory, like the lift could take me anywhere and nobody would ever realise I had vanished.

With a sharp jolt the lift had finally reached its destination on floor six. Stepping out of the lift, I was met with a room that had a couple of comfy armchairs in each corner, a tea tray complete with mugs sat on the floor, along with a small table set between the two chairs. A couple of coats were hanging on a peg, and two navy-blue and white striped cleaner's aprons, so this was more than likely the cleaners' break room. I looked all around me but could not see so much as a cleaning cloth, let alone the bleach and floor mops that were needed. Glancing to my right, I could make out a small staircase, so I headed over to it and climbed up about ten steps until I reached yet another small room. I could just about see around the room, as a small dusty window let in the orange glow of the sun. I grabbed what cleaning stuff I could and turned to leave, but something caught my attention very briefly, and as I looked up, I could see the ancient timber beams helping to support this old building. A few of these beams continued down the sides of the bowed walls as well, and I could just about make out some sets of initials, maybe about five pairs. As I looked closer, I could see that these names were not that old, I would guess ten to fifteen years. The wood was lighter underneath still, much lighter than it would have been if done decades before. Splinters of wood were still sticking out and not worn with age at all.

I wanted to get out of here pronto as this area of the factory seemed to have a soul, breathing almost. It was not really a bad foreboding I was feeling, more so a feeling that eyes were watching me from inside the walls and any minute now I would see a ghost or two. I ran down the few stairs and into the small cleaners' room with a distinct feeling that something or someone was behind me. My arms were full, carrying as much cleaning products as I could. I did not fancy making a return trip anytime soon.

"God that was creepy." I was still looking over my shoulder as I told the girls of the attic room. Of course, they did their normal laughter, thinking it was hilarious that I was the one to be sent up there.

"That is your punishment for leaving us lot to help clean this dump, and you will not get to meet Mr Wonderful. You lucky bugger." The look on Sandra and Maggie's faces spoke volumes.

Did I feel guilty for leaving them? Did I hell. I would have done not so long ago, but I had toughened up a lot of late. "You're big girls now. You will cope," I replied with a wink.

"Yeah. Yeah. Cheers, mate," they both teased back in unison. I did love working with them both, even though they had put the fear of God in me when I first started working here. They had good hearts and were what my grandfather would have called "The salt of the earth". If they liked you, then you were going to be OK, and they would see that you were looked after and stick up for you in your absence. If they did not like you, then you would soon find out, that was for sure.

Putting on my thick winter coat, I was thinking about tea tonight, feeling glad that I had put a stew in the slow cooker that morning. I really was tired out and the last thing that I wanted to do was cook. Heading down the short driveway of the factory, I came across an old lady walking her dog. We got chatting as we were walking in the same direction towards the school. "Have you lived here long?" I asked the lady, just for something to say.

"Oh yes. All my life, dear."

"You must have seen some changes over the years then."

"I have indeed. So many changes, and not all for the better, I am afraid to say." This sweet old lady then went on to tell me that where we were stood was all part of one huge estate many years ago. I explained that I lived just a stone's throw away on the new housing estate. I say new as it was new when we bought our house some fifteen years ago. The old lady nodded, adding that the housing estate, school, doctors' surgery, a small row of shops, and even a forty-bed nursing home were all built at the same time and that whole area was also one huge place, surrounded by farmland and fields, only the factory remained of the original building and outbuilding as the rest was all sold off to developers in the early to mid-eighties.

"What was it all? It must have been massive. Did a wealthy family own it?" I asked her, thinking of all the big stately manor houses I had seen on the television.

"No, nothing like that, dear. It was the old pauper's Victorian lunatic asylum."

The hairs on my arms stood on end. I bid her farewell and left, continuing to the school gates with more questions than answers.

Toby and Millie came rushing up to me and gave me the biggest cuddle, which was most unusual, especially for Toby. "What are you two after then?" I quizzed them suspiciously.

"Miss Tomlin reminded us that its non-school-uniform day tomorrow," Millie said a little sheepishly.

"Oh, did she now. And who did not let me know that then?" This was all I needed, thrust upon me at the last minute.

"We did have a letter about it, Mum," Millie said as sweetly as she could. "That was weeks ago."

I mused as my brain was working overtime trying to recall a letter, as I would normally write such events on the trusted kitchen calendar. "Well, not to worry, you can go in your everyday clothes. It's not like its fancy dress or anything, is it?" I prayed. Wishful thinking.

"We have to dress as our favourite character from a book or film." *This day is just getting better*, I thought to myself.

Arriving home, I double-checked the calendar and, just as I thought, nothing was written down. Emptying their school bags, I came across the usual uneaten fruit festering in the bottom. Why they couldn't leave it in the lunchboxes,

I would never know. I dug deeper and found three screwed-up letters lurking at the very bottom of their bags, smudged and sodden with God knows what, more than likely some forgotten tangerine or apple.

"Kids, can you come in the kitchen, please?" Two faces appeared as if butter would not melt. "Can either of you tell me what this letter was about?" They both looked at each other and then back at me.

"Might have been about the non-school-uniform day." Toby looked at Millie, then they both looked at me.

"Right, you two puddings, up the stairs and get rummaging in your dress-up box."

As I made the dumplings to put in the steaming beef stew, I could not help thinking about the conversation I had had earlier with the old lady. The eerie feeling I'd experienced going up in the lift and in the attic room at work and finding out that our house was built on the land of an old Victorian lunatic asylum. Was it all connected in one way or another? Was this meant to be, me meeting this old lady? I would certainly have a lot to tell Mark when I went for my next session.

"Dinner's nearly ready, you two," I shouted up the stairs. I could hear the two still trying to find something to wear for this non-uniform day tomorrow.

"OK, Mum. We will not be long."

Steve had not long got in from his building job and as he headed up to the shower, I asked him to jolly Millie and Toby along. "Have you found anything to wear yet?" Of course they had not; they had got sidetracked playing with toys that had not seen the light of day for years. "Problem solved. You can both go as Mary and Joseph as it is so near to Christmas," I said, thinking of the pair of striped tea towels that I had in the kitchen cupboard. Feeling pleased with myself at the thought that I had come up with a great and – even better – free idea, I poured Steve and myself a large glass of red wine.

As we all ate dinner that evening, I decided to tell Steve about the conversation that I had had with the old lady and how it felt strange, as if it were all meant to be. Steve scoffed at me, telling me not to believe in that mumbo jumbo and dismissed everything I had told him about my regression sessions with Mark so far. This was just typical of Steve. He only ever saw what was in front of him. If the children and I were OK and he had plenty of work on, and of course he had a good old-fashioned meal to come home to, he was contented with life.

I sat back in my chair, taking another large slug of red wine, and looked over at him mopping up the last of the stew gravy with a piece of dumpling that no doubt he had saved for this very reason. "Got any more, love? That was lovely." He stretched back in his chair, wiping his chin clean of stew. I did love him so.

Later that evening when the kiddos were in bed, we settled down together on the sofa with another glass of red in hand, watching some new drama on the television. Our little room warm and cosy, just the standard light on in the corner. We did not have much, but we were happy with our lot and richer in so many ways than what money could bring. I closed my eyes sleepily, my face flushing warm with the red wine taking effect. "I'm going up to bed, Steve, see you in a while." I started climbing up the wooden hill, looking forward to slinking into my bed.

"OK, love. See you in a bit."

Secretly I wanted to get to bed so I could go over today's events again, let my brain try and figure all of this out. I was convinced it was all related somehow and a power greater than we knew was at work.

Chapter 11

1845

Locking eyes with Esme, I feel a connection that pulls me into her very soul. I sit beside her on the small uncomfortable bed. "I am attendant fourteen. You can either call me that or just call me 'miss' if you like." Esme is deadpan, and although she is looking at me, she is also looking through me. I am shuddering now, and I turn to Doctor Jones, in the hope he will tell me what I should be doing.

One thing that has been drummed into me by all the staff is that I must not under any circumstances get involved with any conversation with the patients about why they have been put in this asylum. Should they try and convince me that they are sane, I am to totally ignore what they are saying by changing the subject.

I am now being told by Doctor Jones to take Esme down the corridor and put her in the dayroom, settle her with a book, or put the gramophone on. Then and only then should I start my observations. The matron is standing next to me, asking if I understand my instruction. I am nodding at her, signalling my understanding. The doctor and matron turn and briskly walk away.

I am more relaxed now that I am alone with Esme, and I can physically see Esme's shoulders relax too. I am telling her that she must be so pleased to be out of the depths of the padded cells, that this means she must be improving. Esme is grabbing my arm tightly, so I look down at her vice-like hands. The whites of her bony knuckles are showing the strength and pressure of this woman's grip. Desperately I am trying to prise her fingers from around my arm.

Feeling panic rise in me, I look around the room for Hairy Mole and Beady Eye. No one is around to help me – only a few patients are in the dayroom with us. Dribbling and shuffling around with slippers that are too big for their feet. I am looking around the room for another aid that may help. Two women are still sat in those armchairs, their noses touching their knees. I am on my own. Terrified. Esme has now loosened her grip slightly and is pulling me towards her.

"You must help me, miss, please," Esme says. I am that close to her I can feel her hair touching the side of my face, I can smell the staleness of her unwashed hair and body. Esme is now telling me that she is not mad and was forced into this asylum against her will.

"I tricked them all into thinking I was mad. They were all trying to poison me back at the village. My mother, my neighbours, my lover, and even my boss."

I am now looking away and try to change the subject, as I have been told to do. I do not want to indulge Esme in her wild fantasies.

"I was brought in by my mother. She is the worst, most evil one of the lot of them."

Esme is becoming agitated, saying that she just wants someone to believe her. And to prove to everyone that she is no lunatic. I look down at my feet, not knowing what to do or say. I am now suggesting she chooses a book to read as it might be a useful distraction. Esme stands up, looking at me with her wild eyes, her unruly hair half sticking to her small face. She is cross, mad as hell. Esme is screaming, swearing with such venom that spit is flying out of her mouth, and now she is running around the dayroom manically. The other women are distressed, and some are wailing and copying Esme. One woman stands up and starts to sing and dance at the top of her lungs. This is upsetting everyone and is certainly adding to Esme's erratic behaviour.

My stomach is turning over, and I want to run away. I do not know what I should do. Relief comes over me as I see Hairy Mole and Beady Eye running into the dayroom, blowing on a silver whistle, which instantly shocks the women into silence, all except Esme, that is. In one swipe the two attendants manage to get Esme onto the floor and sit on top of her. Esme is now out of control, like a wild animal caught in a trap. I cannot see her face. Her hair is covering her wild eyes, and she is now making a low growling sound as if growing tired.

Both Hairy Mole and Beady Eye are not pleased with me, shouting and cursing at me for not keeping Esme under control. I feel the tears threatening to spill from my eyes once more. There is a strange quietness about the dayroom now. The two ladies in the armchairs are now sat upright, grinning at nothing and fiddling with the cloth on their tops. The manic dancer is still dancing but more sedately, twirling around the room as if she is holding an invisible partner in her arms. The other women that stay in the room are sat in the same position as they were before the outburst, talking and laughing to themselves.

"Please do not take Esme away," I now beg the two attendants, and they grin back at me, saying she deserves punishment for behaving in such a way. The dinner bell is now being rung and distracts all thoughts of punishment from their minds.

I am feeling very scared around Esme as I lead her towards the dining room. I ask her why she had the outburst, and she tells me that she feels mad as not one soul will listen to her. "I just need to tell you what happened to me and that it is not me that is mad," she says. Can I trust her? I ask myself. I will be on my guard with her from now on.

We are now entering the dining room, and the smell of boiled cabbage is revolting. The tables are set out in long rows with hardback chairs made of metal. The staff eat in here as well, as I can see the matron and the other superintendents tucking their serviettes into their starched collars. As I walk past their table, the food looks edible and smells as it should.

Once I have settled Esme down in her seat at the table, I am told by Beady Eye to bring the other women through. As had happened earlier that morning, once you tell one patient to go to the dining room, the rest follow like sheep. One by one they follow each other. Some are in pairs, holding hands in a childlike manner. Others are skipping along the corridor. The shufflers are slower and grab at the walls to steady themselves. Then there is Gertie, looking lost and frightened. I now ask her to come with me as it is dinner time. Gertie is walking around in circles and making a strange grunting sound, holding her back end, and saying, "Please. Please, miss." I do not know what is wrong with this frail old lady, other than she is in a state of high distress. I take her by her arm and lead her towards the dining room. Gertie stops in her tracks and relief floods over her face, if only for a brief time, before she then begins wailing and crying. I can smell and see instantly why. Gertie has been incontinent and is in a mess.

Hairy Mole is heading our way now and grabs Gertie from me. "Clean that up, girl. Now." I am being barked at by old Beady Eye, who tells Gertie she will have to stay like that until she learns to go to the toilet. The smell is making me gag. I try to breathe through my mouth as I am on my hands and knees, scrubbing the faeces from the carpet.

I am now back in the dining room and the noise is loud, cutlery being scraped on plates or being thrown on the floor. Cups banging on the hard wooden tables, some women protesting about the food, some just staring at the congealed cold food on their plates – they either cannot or will not eat it. I peer over to Esme. She is not eating or drinking anything at all. I am walking over towards Gertie now; she must eat something as she will die before long. I pick up some sort of watery gloop on the spoon, bits of grey fatty-looking scrag ends of meat, runny potatoes with grey lumps in them, the almost disintegrated cabbage, and what looks like gravy. The smell is just awful. I can see grease floating on the top of the gravy. I am being told the meal is lamb, and I should sit down and eat mine as I will not be getting anything else all day. The pudding looks a little more pleasing, rice pudding with a dollop of jam in the middle. I am pleading with both Esme and Gertie to eat a little bit of pudding. I take some sugar from the kitchen side and put two big spoonfuls into Gertie's pudding, giving it a stir. I lift the spoon carefully to Gertie's mouth and she opens it like a little baby bird. I am looking around me, terrified of getting caught by Beady Eye or Hairy Mole, as I have already been told not to feed Gertie. Her little mouth is opening before I am ready with the next spoonful, the warm milky pudding and jam dripping off her chin.

It is my turn to serve the cups of tea from the big teapot. Milk and sugar have already been added, so if you do not take sugar, you go without. Is this because it adds to the patient's nutrition or is it just done out of pure laziness? I wonder. Stopping at Gertie and Esme's table, I pour them both a cup of tea, instructing them to drink up. Leaning over, I help Gertie to take hold of her cup and lift it to her open mouth. Gertie thinks it is more pudding, so the tea spills from her mouth. At this Gertie looks terrified, so I tell her not to worry as I mop up the tea. I glance over to Esme and I am shocked to see that she is smiling at me, the most kindest smile I have received in a very long time. Her eyes light up and her smile alters her whole face. Esme really is quite beautiful. I pass Esme now to encourage her to drink her cup of tea. Esme looks up at me, taking my hand very gently in hers, and whispers softly, "I am sorry for frightening you, miss." I give her hand a gentle squeeze back. A tender moment is shared between us, and her eyes are pleading to tell me something.

A black bin sits inside the kitchen door where all the slops get scraped into. The sight is repulsive and, combined with the smell, turns my stomach inside out. Plate after plate is being poured into this bin, and blow flies are already hovering nearby. All this food is going for pig's swill on the farm which is attached to this asylum. I really do not want to eat my dinner but know I should as I will need the energy for the rest of the gruelling day ahead.

I am being ordered to collect all the cups now off the tables, then it is time to settle the women back down in the dayroom after we have directed them to the toilet. I glance over at Esme, and I cannot believe what I am seeing. Esme is tenderly feeding Gertie her cup of tea. I feel a rush of love for them both as I think of doing this very same thing to my own mother.

Is this the act of a dangerous lunatic? I ask myself. I now know that I need to find out what happened to Esme. It is time she was listened too, at least by one person anyway.

"That is enough for today, May. It is time to come back to the present day. I will count down from three and you will be back in the room, safe. Three, two, one, you are back with me. Goodness me, that was a deep session, May. I don't think I have ever had anyone go as in-depth as you did today."

Making certain I was fully awake and compos mentos, Mark let me go on my way. "See you next week, Mark," I trilled as I left the room. I had a spring in my step.

Chapter 12

1995

I decided to give Colin a call to see how he was doing. He still sounded rough, as his voice was hoarse, and you could tell his sinuses were blocked.

"How is it going, Colin? Feeling any better?" I hoped that he was as we could really do with him back in work.

"Yes, feeling a lot better and should be back at work in the morning, all being well," he replied, adding as an afterthought, "I bet my name's been mud, hasn't it?"

"No, not at all, Colin, of course it hasn't. Everyone has been very concerned and understanding," I lied, crossing my fingers.

"OK, May, thanks for ringing. See you in the morning then." Poor Colin sounded how I felt about that sweatshop we called work.

Tomorrow was going to be a good day. Not only did I have my mate Colin back into the fold, but it was Thursday and that meant my next regression session with Mark. When the alarm sounded, I stretched and groaned, but I got out of my bed with a bit more enthusiasm than normal. After the usual mad panic of waking my two little cherubs up, it was downstairs to start the onslaught of breakfast, lunchbox packing, and everything else in between. Kids fed and watered, it was a quick dash upstairs to make sure that the flannels and toothbrushes were wet, which proved their faces and hopefully bodies had seen some sort of soap and water this morning. Kids all set to go, including stripy tea towels on heads, we were off out the door. I was in such a good mood I could hardly believe myself. Even Lucinda could not dampen my light mood as she gushed the usual sickly sweet "Good morning, hun," looking as drop-dead gorgeous as usual.

"Hi, Lucinda. Cannot stop. Running late." I did not want her to spoil my good mood.

"OK, sweet pea, catch you soon," I heard her trill in the distance.

Stood in their normal spot were Maggie and Sandra, dragging the life out of no doubt their second ciggie in ten minutes. "Hiya, May. Are you ready for another day in paradise?" Sandra said to me at the same time as inhaling her Benson & Hedges.

"Yes, can't wait," I sarcastically replied, adding, "Colin is back in today. Go easy on him though, please, as he will be feeling a bit sheepish. He thinks that his name is mud with all of us having to work extra."

Maggie replied, "Of course we will. Goes without saying, doesn't it, Sandra." To which Sandra nodded her agreement. Suddenly Maggie yelled at the top of her voice across the yard. "Here he comes. Hiya, mud," she called, closely followed by, "Here comes sick note." Both women clung to each other laughing.

"What are you calling me mud for?" enquired Colin.

"Well, that is your name, isn't it? You said I bet your name is mud, so there you go, mud."

God please no. I could have crawled away and disappeared as it was more than obvious that I had told them what he had said. How mortifyingly embarrassing. Colin glared at me before sloping off into the factory like a scolded cat. "Thanks a bunch, you two. Why did you say that? He is going to hate me now."

"Oh, chill out, May. We are only having a laugh," Sandra said, still wiping the tears of laughter from her cheeks.

"Yes, at my expense. I cannot believe you both did that." Still feeling embarrassed, I made my way through the factory doors, my good mood fading fast. I had to clear the air with Colin. I bet he thought I was a right two-faced old cow. I found Colin lurking in the small kitchen, making himself a cup of coffee. "Colin, I am so sorry about that. I was just asking them to go easy on you and not to tease you as you were worried your name was mud." Colin turned around to face me, and I could tell that his cold must have been nasty as he still had the remnants of old scabs around his top lip and the edge of one nostril. "Please forgive me, Colin. I would never in a million years do anything to upset you."

Giving his nose an extra blow along with a little cough to boot, he said, "That is OK, May. We will say no more about it."

"Thank you, Colin," I gratefully replied. I just hoped that Tweedledee and Tweedledum kept their mouths shut now as well.

I just had time to go up to the cleaning room again. I needed to see it one more time. Plucking up the courage, I asked Nancy if I could quickly go up to the room in the lift, as I thought that I might have lost my bracelet up there yesterday. "For goodness' sake, May, be quick then. You have five minutes." She tapped at her beloved wristwatch as if setting a timer for a race, adding bitterly, "If you are not back in five minutes, I shall be docking it out of your wages. That lift is not a fun fair ride, you know." The fun-loving free-spirited party animal that we saw several weeks ago had certainly shrivelled back to work Nancy again.

"What a cow," I cursed under my breath. As I reached the top floor of the attic, I felt more confident than the last time. Sadly I also felt nothing at all when I was up there. No divine intervention. No ghost of the past. Nothing. Whatever I had felt yesterday was not there today. Back down to the factory floor I went, feeling a little bit despondent to say the least. Probably wishful thinking, I concluded. Talk soon turned to the normal gossip on the production line, who was sleeping with who and who was going to make the biggest fool of themselves at the impending Christmas do. I was just happy that Colin was being left alone.

Later in the morning, just before our 10am tea break, we were all summoned by Nancy and instructed to "Gather round, ladies, and Colin." Nancy was standing proud, handing out some sort of paperwork and, by the looks of it, looking very pleased with herself. As we all formed an orderly queue awaiting our turn, Colin had worked out what it was declaring.

"I bet you anything it's the menu for our Christmas party, and we have to choose our food."

"I thought for a minute Nancy was in the midst of handing out OBEs. I was getting ready to curtsy at one point," I said sarcastically with a grin.

Sandra and Maggie were itching to grab their menus as all this messing about was cutting into their precious fag break. Once outside Maggie declared, "Cor, have a look at the choices on the menu. It all looks dead posh, don't it?"

Sandra had already made her choice, adding, "Looks like a posh place, have to wear our best bib and tucker that night."

"Seems the old chap Bonner is pushing the boat out this year, don't it?" Maggie could hardly hold her excitement in. The prospect of a Christmas party and a three-course meal, plus a disco and wine on the table, nearly pushed her over the edge. I glanced at this piece of paper that was causing all this excitement, and I must admit it did all look nice. For starter you could have the choice of seasonal soup, which was melon, pâté on Melba toast, or prawn cocktail. Then for the main course it was salmon with seasonal vegetables and buttered new potatoes. Roast beef with all the trimmings in a red wine gravy. Nut loaf and seasonal vegetables, no doubt for any vegetarians. Or the good old-fashioned roast turkey with all the trimmings. The puddings looked equally as tempting too. Christmas pudding with either custard, brandy butter, or ice cream. Chocolate fudge cake with seasonal fruit served with cream. Strawberry cheesecake served with cream or ice cream. Or lastly, just ice cream. All polished off with a mince pie at the end if you had room, of course. I was feeling slightly more enthusiastic about things now, plus the Christmas do would also signify the impending two-week shut-down of the factory. Two whole weeks at home with my family. Bliss.

"Did you know that this building and the local housing estate and complex use to be an old Victorian lunatic asylum?" I asked Maggie and Sandra when we were back on our line.

"Where have you been, May? Living under a blimmin' rock? How did you not know that?" Sandra said, almost sounding exasperated with me for not knowing.

I tried in vain to explain that I was not from this area originally. Of course, that was ignored as Maggie piped up, saying, "God yes, it was one hell of a place years ago. Had its own farm, laundry, kitchen, chapel, and even its own morgue."

Up until this point Colin had stayed quiet, only this conversation piqued his interest, so he joined in the talk. "I heard it was haunted and even to this day ghosts of the past staff and patients can be heard and seem around these parts."

My ears pricking up, I just had to ask, "Have you ever seen a ghost around here or on the estate, Colin?"

He gave me a sideways glance, replying, "No, not me, but my nan always reckoned she used to see ghosts over the years. She lived in an old cottage down in the village. Both the cottage and my nan are long gone now though."

Maggie butted in. "Colin, don't know about your nan seeing a ghost, but I bet she's seen some spirits in her time." That sent both women into raptures of laughter again.

"What about you two then, ever seen or heard anything odd?"

"Only my old man first thing in the morning, now that is a bloody odd sight, let me tell you." We all laughed, Sandra and Maggie the loudest though.

"Seriously though, have you never heard or seen anything at all? It is such an old building, and the surrounding area must have so much history attached to it."

"Nah, not me, but one of the nighttime cleaners won't go upstairs on her own, reckons she saw something once."

"What did she see, Maggie?" I asked eagerly.

"Oh, I don't know, some old gal in some sort of uniform, I think. Wasn't it, Sandra?"

"Yes, something like that," Sandra added half-heartedly.

"The best person you could ask would be Nancy. Didn't her mother or grandmother work there at some point, Sandra?"

"So the story goes, Maggie. She doesn't like talking about it for some reason," Sandra added, but she didn't know any more than that.

"Have to get her drunk at the Christmas do, May," Maggie suggested with a wild twinkle in her hazel eyes.

All this talk of ghosts from the asylum made me think that just maybe I had not imagined feeling like I was being watched when I went up to the attic that day. All I knew was that something was wrong up there. That room had a heavy, repressive feeling about it, and I was determined to find out more. The more I was learning about Esme and the other patients, the more I was convinced that one of them was trying to tell me something. And I was not going to give up the ghost, so to speak, until I found out just what that was.

77

Chapter 13

1845

The walls feel and look even more wet and miserable this morning, like they themselves are crying tears. The glow of the lamps illuminate the long streaks of damp. Walking into the ward, I jump and shriek as a rat runs from under one bed across to the other. This reaction at once wakes and unsettles the patients. I am trying to calm them all down before Hairy Mole and Beady Eye come into the ward.

Gertie is sat on the edge of her bed just as she was the morning before, fiddling with the hem of her grey nightgown. One woman is screaming hysterically, pulling at her hair. I go over to this poor soul, offering a bit of comfort and to see if I can help her. She is now spitting and frothing at the mouth, her limbs are jerking and going rigid, blood is pouring from her mouth, though I can't see where from.

Hairy Mole is now in the room. I look over at the door and I can see only her face in the light of the lamp, which wears a scowl. Her top lip is inside her mouth, and she is making that sucking sound on it again. Her hair is tightly scraped off her face so only her wrinkled forehead is showing, making her look even more stern than she is. She is coming closer to me and the woman now. She is not happy at all and grabs this woman's arm tightly and tells her to stop. This woman is taking no notice whatsoever.

"Right then, Elsie, you have left me no choice but to give you the cold-water therapy. See if that will make you see sense and bring you out of your devilish trance."

I am told to go with Beady Eye and get the bath ready. The bath stands in the middle of the room and is being filled with stone-cold water. I am chilled to the bone just looking at it, my feet and hands have gone white, and I am visibly shaking with both fear and cold. Beady Eye is now bringing over some tortuous-looking equipment. It has two mechanisms attached to it and then a white sheet is brought into the room as well.

Elsie is guided into the bathroom now by Hairy Mole and another young attendant who I do not recognise. They are wheeling her in on a wooden chair on wheels, and the young attendant is laying across Elsie to stop her falling out the contraption. Elsie is still jerking, spitting, and frothing at the mouth, her grey nightgown drenched with both blood and spit. Her eyes are rolling back in her head so only the whites of her eyes are showing. Elsie is making an inaudible grunting noise.

Hairy Mole is now fighting to get Elsie undressed. I watch both Hairy Mole and Beady Eye lifting Elsie swiftly and putting the white sheet underneath her body. They are connecting her to the thing with two arms and are now lowering Elsie into the freezing-cold bath. At once Elsie stops breathing from the shock of the icy water hitting her body. For a few seconds all is still, and I am certain Elsie is dead. The seconds feel like hours. Elsie takes a huge breath, her arms and legs flailing around her, spilling water across the stone floor and turning the colour of the stone from light grey to dark grey. At last Elsie is calmer and taking in deep breaths of air, her eyes are back in her head, and she is trying to focus on us and on the room. The three attendants seem pleased that this treatment has worked again to bring Elsie back to how she should be. The young attendant is asking questions about Elsie, and I open my ears so as not to miss a word. Beady Eye is explaining that Elsie was brought into the asylum as she was showing signs of madness and hysteria. Once a month when her curse happens upon her, she has these episodes.

"The devil has got inside her, and this is Elsie showing how he can control her. The blood is where she bites her tongue, the devil's mark." Hairy Mole is now telling the young attendant that Elsie and her husband have been trying to have a baby, and this is being hindered by the devil, making her curse come as he enters her body and takes over her soul. "This treatment is the only hope for Elsie, a cure which is working. The second we submerge her in the water, the hysteria stops, as the devil leaves her body. Once Elsie is fully cured, she can go back home to her husband, and she will be with child."

I am now being told by Beady Eye to "Get the bucket and mop, girl, and clean this mess up." I am doing as I am told and going along what seems like miles of corridors. Twisting and turning this way and that, each turn I take has a concave archway. The walls cry more tears than ever the deeper I venture.

I am now stood at a small stairwell with stone steps going up into darkness. These steps are smaller and much thinner than any of the others that I have seen since being here. I am now right up to the top of the stairs; my eyes are having trouble focusing on anything until they adjust to the dark. My hands are feeling all around me, and I am nearly tripping over things I cannot see.

Now my eyes are acclimatised, I can see the tin bucket stood in the left-hand corner of the room. The mop is sitting in the bucket, and as I get nearer, I can see filthy dirty water within. A stagnant smell is emitting from the mop head, which looks like it is made from old torn-up towels. The water in the bucket is brown and sludgy like ditch water. I am suddenly taken back to the stream that my brothers and I would play in for hours on end. With our jam jars in hand, we would paddle in the stream and scoop up the water in jars, trying to catch the passing sticklebacks and minnows. We would take a jam sandwich with us as most likely we would be gone all day. What I wouldn't give more than anything to taste one of my dear mother's homemade jam sandwiches. Resting by the stream, laying in the sweet-smelling grass that would gently tickle our legs, we took in the sounds of the skylarks and song thrushes singing their joyful tune. I cannot stop the tears now from coming down my face. Oh, how I wish I could see my family just one more time.

Lugging the pail of dirty water down the dark stone staircase is difficult. The steps are thin and some of the stone is crumbling away. My knees and back are feeling the strain as I try not to fall. Back downstairs in the freezing bathroom, I can see that Elsie is now out of the bathtub and is dressed and sat back in the wooden chair on wheels. Her pallor is looking better. Elsie looks dazed and confused as if she has no idea of what has happened or even where she is. "Get this mopped up quick, girl, and no dilly-dallying. We got lunatics to get ready," Hairy Mole is bellowing at me. I am thinking to myself how I despise the word "lunatic". These are people with names, that had lives and a family before being received into the asylum. Where is the love? Where is the compassion and care?

Now that I have mopped the floor, I must use some tatty old towels to make the stone dry and help it return to its original colour pre-bath. I look at my hands, which have gone from numb white to mottled blue and red, yet my face is feeling hot from all the mopping and drying. I feel the sweat forming on my forehead and just beneath my nose. The water on the floor is ice-cold. By the time I am done, all the patients are up and dressed and are in the dining room eating breakfast.

I am now passing Gertie, who I know has not been washed as I can easily smell the ammonia emitting from her. Sat by the side of Gertie is Esme, lovingly spooning the grey watery slop into Gertie's open mouth. "I put extra sugar in it, miss. Just like you did yesterday," Esme is telling me proudly. I thank Esme, telling her that was a thoughtful thing to do. Gertie seems unaware of who is helping her to eat or what indeed it is, just opening her mouth like a tiny bird.

I am now feeling that I need to get to know Esme and her story. "Do you like to read, Esme?" I ask her as I start to wipe the tables down after breakfast.

"I cannot read, miss," Esme replies.

"Can you pretend to read, do you think?" I ask in a quiet voice so as not to raise suspicion from Beady Eye.

"I can try, miss. Why?" Esme has a confused look on her face, not understanding yet what my idea is.

My idea is to get permission from the matron and the superintendent to let me sit with Esme whilst she reads a book or at least pretends to. I will tell the superintendent that Esme has shown an interest in reading, and I think that is a good thing as it has a calming effect on the patient. They both think that it is a brilliant idea. My plan has worked and very soon I can bring it into fruition.

"Pick a book that you think you might like, please, Esme. Make sure it is a large volume of a book as I think we might be a while." Esme duly follows my instruction and chooses a book. Sitting down now on the small two-seater settee, I open the book to the first page. Handing it over to Esme, I explain how she can now start telling me her story and all that has happened to lead to her being here in the asylum. "You see, Esme, as you look at the book and slowly turn the pages, you won't be reading, but pretending to read, and in fact you will be telling me your story." Esme smiles at me, understanding just what I mean.

So, on a dark foggy afternoon, I am allowed ten minutes with Esme. The story has begun. Esme is telling me that she was just a young innocent girl desperate to find work, her parents making her go her own way now that she was older. After being employed as a scullery maid at a large home in the local town, it soon became clear that Esme was being treated unkindly by the head cook in the kitchen. Esme knew that the work would be hard and gruelling but did not expect the harsh treatment that was put upon her. Her day would start at 5am, when she would black lead the grate, relay the fire in the kitchen, then light it, making sure it was well stoked and carrying coal in from the coal shed. Then she swept the floor of the kitchen and peeled vegetables ready for her master and mistress's lunch. All this had to be done before 8am. The head cook always found fault with whatever Esme had done. The black leading wasn't done well enough, the fire not built up with kindling high enough, even the vegetables were cut too thick or too thin for the cook's liking. She scolded Esme with harsh words, "stupid girl" or "imbecile" to name but a few. Very often these harsh remarks would be followed by a slap around her head as well. Cook would prepare the master's breakfast, which usually consisted of smoked haddock with bread and butter, with the mistress preferring eggs and toast. Cook would sometimes make a little extra food for herself and the other kitchen maids, but Esme was never once offered any food. A scullery maid was the lowest of the lowest jobs, but it was better than starving on the streets or, worse still, at the workhouse. At least Esme had a roof over her head and a bed to sleep upon, food, and her board was also included in the agreement when she took the job on.

One morning Esme had laid the fire up ready for another day, and a young man entered the kitchen. This young man introduced himself as Percy and told Esme that he was the stable hand. He wanted something to eat and drink as he was feeling faint from hunger and cold. Going over to the large teapot that was keeping warm on top of the stove, Esme poured him some tea and cut him a slice of bread that Cook had left out on the side. She also sneaked a chunk of cheese into his hand, telling him to go or else Cook would have her guts for garters. This early morning visit soon became a regular arrangement, and not long after, Esme was developing a soft spot for Percy, falling in love with him. At nighttime when the moon was shining bright, Esme recalls how they would meet up in the courtyard and sit together on a nearby wrought iron seat, gazing at the twinkling stars, trying to find and name all the different planets. The stars shone bright like diamonds in the frosty night air. One night they went on a walk across some fields and settled down on Percy's coat, which he had laid on the damp grass for them both. It was near a river with a sandy bank leading down into shallow water.

Esme stops talking now, her eyes far away and misting over. "We will leave it for today, Esme. We can read again tomorrow."

"May, that's enough for this evening. I am bringing you back to the safety of my room. The fire is warm, and the letter opener is in front of you. Open your eyes slowly. Three, two, one, open your eyes, May. You are back in 1995."

I took longer to come back this time. As I found out more about my earlier life and the connection I felt with Esme was getting stronger, I wanted to stay longer and longer each time. Whatever it was that gave Esme a faraway look in her eyes and stop talking, I feared it would be traumatic for her to recall and for me to hear.

Chapter 14

1995

I was so tired the morning after my session I felt almost drugged and in a dream-like state. I was also now dreaming of both May and Esme; it was consuming me. The feeling that I had was so powerful I felt certain that all would become clear in the end, and possibly alter the path of my life. I could not pinpoint what this would be, only that I felt it in my bones that it would happen.

It was Saturday morning and Steve had taken Toby to an early football match in the next town. Millie had slept over at her friend's and the girl's mother was going to be taking them to the cinema and a burger restaurant for a birthday treat for her daughter. So, I was a lady of leisure – well, for an hour anyway. I had to go into town to pick this dreaded Secret Santa present. Worst case scenario had happened, and I had drawn the short straw. Guess who I got? Nancy. Just my luck. What should I buy her? She was like two different people, the staunch, sensible supervisor versus the party animal downing Pernod and blackcurrant like it was going out of fashion. Now which Nancy to buy for was my conundrum for this morning. I had asked Maggie and Sandra, but as usual they had found my whole predicament hilarious and were no help whatsoever. Next, I asked Colin if he had any suggestions. His response was just a shake of his head. I think Colin could not care less what I bought Nancy; he was just relieved it wasn't him who pulled that name out of the bag. Just my bloody luck.

I finished my tea and toast and headed to the bus stop to catch the next bus into town. I needed to pick a few other bits up as well and have a mooch around the shops while I had the chance. It was a freezing morning with a heavy frost, the type of cold that is often explained as biting. The tip of my nose stung with cold despite pulling my woollen scarf up over my mouth. I hoped the bus wouldn't be too long. The sooner I finished, the sooner I could be back home. I thought of the nice tomato soup and warm crusty roll I had promised myself, followed by putting my feet up with a hot water bottle and fleecy blanket, watching some cheesy Christmas film on Channel 5. The housework could wait until tomorrow. I heard the bus before I saw it, chugging up the hill. Thank goodness it had arrived; I wanted to get on and warm up. It was only a short trip into town, ten minutes on a good day. Today I would not have minded it taking longer so I could stay in the warm a little bit longer. I really was feeling chilled through to the bone.

What could I buy? I mused in one of the many department stores. We had a fiver to spend and should not go under or over. Perfume? Toiletries set? A book voucher? Chocolates? A whip? I thought, laughing to myself. The latter felt much more appropriate and would certainly cause a stir. I could just see Maggie and Sandra's faces. They would love it and be besides themselves with laughter, the table wine flying from all directions out of their mouths. Instead of the whip I decided on the sensible choice of a pretty pair of gold earrings with a tiny fake ruby set into each one. I had about a pound left, so I bought a large bar of Cadbury chocolate. Can't go wrong with chocolate, can you?

With that out of the way, I could put it out of my mind. I wanted to get a few little bits and bobs for Toby and Millie's stockings. They were great kids, and I liked to treat them at Christmas. They had their moments like all children but overall were very thoughtful and kind. We didn't go mad at Christmas, as for one thing we couldn't afford it, and for another, I always thought less was more. As a child our family had very little, so at Christmas time my mum always made sure we had a small stocking with lots of small gifts in, all wrapped up individually in the most wonderful, colourful seventies Christmas paper. It did not have to be expensive, a bar of sweet-smelling soap, a flannel, a small bottle of children's perfume, a few plastic toys, and of course the best bit for me was finding the orange bar of chocolate at the bottom of the stocking. We always had a main present as well, either the latest board game, Tiny Tears doll, or pram. It was such a magical time of my life and something that I wanted to recreate with my own children. The simple things in life often made the best memories, the chocolate gold-wrapped coins, decorating the Christmas tree, and taking turns each year to put the fairy or star on top. Adding chocolate coins to the tree on Christmas Eve was always my favourite as I knew the next day would be Christmas Day.

Bringing me out of my sentimental daydream, I felt a gentle tap on my shoulder. "Hello again, dear." It was the little old lady that I had met a few days before.

"Hello, my name is May, by the way. Nice to see you again." I smiled back.

"You too, dear. My name is Gladys."

After a brief chat consisting of small talk, I plucked up the courage to ask her how much she remembered about the old asylum.

"Not a great deal, my dear. We did not work there or anything and our family never attended any of the social evenings that would be put on twice a year. It was a very scary place for us local kids growing up, and we were always warned not to go near the asylum." I was intrigued to know why as a young child she and others had been warned to stay away. "It was not a safe or nice place back in those days. Our parents didn't want us near it. They thought an escapee might grab us and take us into the depths of the asylum, never to be seen or heard of again. It was like that back then, dear. Country folk thought differently from what we do nowadays. In the later years of the old asylum, things improved massively. The patients were treated as human beings and not monsters." Although I did not find out anything of great historical importance, at least I knew that the patients were eventually treated with more kindness and respect than I had experienced in my regression sessions. I hoped I would get to see these changes, or at the very least the beginning of better things to come.

Carrying on with my shopping, I was suddenly hit with the most wonderful smell of freshly made mince pies. The smell was coming from a café in the precinct. I thought, why not treat myself? That didn't happen very often, except on our walk to the park on a Sunday, but never on my own. I felt like a rest, so in I went, deciding on a cup of tea and a hot mince pie.

"Eat in or take away?" the young girl serving asked me as if she was sick to death of repeating the same question.

"Eat in, please," I replied, eyeing up what table to sit at.

"Would you like a biscuit while you wait?" the young girl asked, adding, "We have some complementary ones today as it's near Christmas."

"No, thanks," I replied. I was sick to the back teeth of biscuits. Working with them all day long, the last thing I wanted to do was eat one on my day off.

I took a seat by the window and a young server brought over my cup of tea and welcome mince pie. After I had thanked her, I sat back in my seat, watching all the other shoppers outside. Some were on their own like me, others were in clusters, chatting away and having a catch-up. One middle-aged couple walked by scowling at each other. I could just tell they had argued over something – married women of my age knew that look extremely well. One young couple walked on by hand in hand, the young pretty girl looking up into her handsome boyfriend's eyes. They kissed then shared a joke together in the throes of young love. I smiled to myself at the memory.

Sat in the café to my right was an elderly couple. They were not talking very much, but you could feel and see the love between them, the way he helped her open the sugar sachet that had come with her cup of tea or coffee, the gentle smile she gave him in way of thanks. A group of around four young teenagers were sat to my left, giggling and chatting about the latest pop song or boy they liked, no doubt. They looked so free and happy, and I wondered if this was their first trip out together on their own without Mum or Dad, imagining the anguish and worry their mums would be feeling, hoping that they were safe. Not relaxing until they were safely back at home.

Just then a young mother came in with her toddler, followed by either her husband or boyfriend. The man went up to the till to place their order whilst the young mum and toddler found a seat. Almost immediately the young child started to wriggle, trying to free itself from the mother's lap. I knew instinctively what was bound to come next, for I too had been in this position with my two Herberts a few years before. As if on cue, the high-pitched screaming started, that ear piercing sort that rattles your brain. I closed my eyes and shuddered at the sudden noise. The poor young mum was mortified as she could not have missed all the other customers' eyes looking over. Poor lady. I felt her pain. I could now see that the toddler was a little girl with tight blonde curls. The mother had the writhing, wriggling girl on one hip, jostling her up and down in the hope that it would calm her. The little girl was crying so much that her dummy was half out of her mouth, and she was pushing with all her might against her mother's chest, trying to free herself and run amok in the café. Her face was rosy now and she was not giving up the fight just yet. "Hurry up and get that Mr Blobby biscuit, Trevor, for gawd sake," the woman shouted across the café. Trevor looked at them and nodded, almost wanting to ignore the show that his daughter was putting on. Soon all was calm as the little girl took the Mr Blobby biscuit in her chubby fingers and started sucking the life out of it.

I loved people watching and I could sit here quite happily all day watching the different people from different walks of life come and go. Another couple entered with a little boy. The mum was heavily pregnant, the dad helping her to ease into the small café chair. It put me in mind of our family when we were just starting out and got me thinking about how I met Steve.

I was sixteen and had not long left school. I got a job in the local shop near where I lived. In those days youngsters rarely went to college and it was almost unheard of to go to university. That was for the rich kids that lived in the big detached houses across town. They would more than likely go on to be doctors or solicitors and they certainly wouldn't have gone to my local run-of-the-mill comprehensive, that's for sure. It was whilst I was working in the shop that I met Steve. He had come in for a bag of crisps and a can of coke whilst he was on his dinner break from his job as an apprentice bricklayer. I was on the tills that day, so I served him. His first words to me were "Cheer up, love, it might never happen." Now for anyone reading this, you will know that these words make you feel anything but cheery. It certainly didn't make me feel endeared to him on that very first meeting. I remembered scowling at him as I handed him his change and him saying to me, "Thanks, darlin'. Aren't you a little ray of sunshine." With that he gave me a cocky grin and a wink and ambled out of the shop with a confident swagger. I had to admit he was good-looking in a "Don't I know it" sort of way. He had the confidence of a man older than his years.

"Blimmin' cheeky sod," I mumbled under my breath. I am not a miserable person by nature; I just have one of those resting faces that screams "I'm fed up and miserable".

I am in fact an incredibly happy contented person, that is until someone says, "Cheer up!"

The very next day I was called into my boss's office, well, the crowded box room out the back of the shop. My boss was called Mr Gaskill. He was around sixty years of age at a rough guess, a stout, portly man with the biggest stomach I had ever seen, his shirt buttons straining with every outward breath. His braces that he wore to keep his trousers from falling off his belly only seemed to draw my attention more to his bulbous middle. He had white fluffy hair along with a stubbly beard and wore little dark-rimmed glasses that just framed his small, round blue eyes. Along with a pitted squat nose that had fine blue and red veins threading through it, he also had an extremely high colour. Looking back now, I couldn't help but wonder if he was a heavy drinker or had undetected high blood pressure. "I have had a complaint about you, May," Gaskill informed me. This surprised me as I had always tried to be polite and was never intentionally rude to anyone. "Yes, I am afraid so, May. A complaint has been made about your attitude. Now as this a one-off incident and I have never had to speak with you before this, we will say no more about it."

"Thank you, Mr Gaskill." I was fuming as I had a jolly good idea who this complaint had come from. That cocky coke and crisps builder bloke. *Just you wait until I see him.*

I did not have to wait long until I had my chance to have it out with him. "Why did you make a complaint about me to my boss?" Of course he denied it, promising that it wasn't him. I was still moaning to myself about it a few days later when Mr Gaskill came from out the back.

"What's up, May? You're not still festering on what that Mavis said about you, are you?"

"Mavis? I thought it was that builder bloke, Steve."

"No, I thought I had told you it was Mavis. And to take it with a pinch of salt." Mr Gaskill had certainly not said anything of the sort. He was getting old and forgetful. Had

I known it was Mavis from down the street, then of course I would not have taken a blind bit of notice. You see, Mavis was known locally as Mrs Moan as that was all she ever did. I owed Steve an apology – begrudgingly, I might add. And the rest, as they say, is history.

Being brought out of my daydream by the clatter of someone dropping their cutlery, it was time for me to get a move on. By now the café had filled up with people coming in for their lunch. It was very warm in the café now, so much so that the windows had steamed up. Looking at my watch, I just had time to nip into the supermarket to pick something up for tea.

Maggie and Sandra were working like the clappers Monday morning. Colin and I could hardly keep up the pace. "Slow down, you two," I pleaded. "We can't go that fast." It fell on deaf ears, of course. They went on like this until dinner break. As I was making the tea, I said, "Please can you two take your feet off the pedal this afternoon? It is making my head spin."

Colin was an incredibly quiet chap and a very observant one. He leaned over to me. "They are working like trojans, May. You know why, don't you?" I stared at him blankly until suddenly the penny well and truly dropped.

"The crafty pair of so-and-sos. I thought that was odd and not like them to put themselves out and work more unless they absolutely had to." The cunning pair were after a Christmas bonus and would no doubt be getting it.

No gasping for two ciggies per break today; a quick puff and Maggie ordered, "Come on. Better get back to it." That would soon change after the Christmas break. Normal service would resume; I could guarantee it.

"What did you get the old battleaxe then?" Sandra asked later that afternoon. I made the fatal mistake of telling them. "How boring is that, May. For goodness' sake you could have got her something jokey." Sandra tutted.

"Like what, for instance? I don't think Nancy would appreciate a jokey present. I had to play it safe," I reasoned.

"You could have got her a willy soap on a rope or a pair of fluffy handcuffs," Maggie butted in. "I'm disappointed in you, May. You have let the side down."

Well, I cannot help that, I thought. "Nancy would not even know it was from you. That is the whole point of secret Santa, May. Come on, keep up." They were both glaring at me now. I couldn't seem to do right for doing wrong.

"Why don't you get her a rude and jokey present then, Maggie?" I looked across to see Maggie's response.

"That is not a bad idea, May. Not a bad idea at all. Cheers." Me and my big mouth. Why didn't I just keep quiet? My mind was all over the place today, as I was going to see Mark later that evening instead of going Thursday. My chance to escape for a while. And I could not wait.

Chapter 15

1845

"Tell me what happened to you, Esme. Tell me what happened that night down by the sandy banks of the River Windrush?"

"I had arranged to meet Percy down by the riverbank at 9pm. It was dark outside, but the fields were lit by the moonlight, creating an easy path to navigate. We kissed and hugged, so pleased to see each other. The floor was damp, and Percy took off his coat and laid it down on top of the wet grass. We sat and talked for a while about anything and nothing, the river glimmering in the light of the full moon. Percy took my face in his hands and held my gaze. I can see just how beautiful his dark brown eyes are. His soft clear skin looks like porcelain. He took my chin with a gentle hand and lifted it up further to his face. We were close now, so close that I could see the Cupid's bow of his perfect lips. We kissed, a passionate kiss, and Percy whispered to me how long he had wanted to kiss me. He kissed me some more, on my lips, my forehead, and even my nose before his lips were snaking down my neck.

"He was now sat before me on his knees, unbuttoning my blouse and undoing my undergarments. Percy was fondling my naked breast, milk white and bare for anyone passing by to see. I did not care, as I was so absolutely in love with this wonderful young man. Percy lowered me down onto his coat and laid beside me, resting his head on his hand. Staring into my eyes, he told me how pretty I was, how he had never felt this way about anyone else before. Telling me how we would be married and be so wonderfully happy together for the rest of our lives on earth and beyond.

Then he took my hand in his and guided it towards his man parts. He was ready for me, and he moved his body towards mine. I was scared. I was nervous. I was an untouched pure woman. I was a virgin.

"I gave myself to Percy willingly that night beside the sandy riverbank in the full light of the moon. Although I did not fully understand what was happening, I did understand that it must be how a man and woman showed their committed love to each other. As we walked back hand in hand, the large house came into view. Percy had his own room above the stables and mine was above the kitchen, a large square courtyard between us. The night had a slight chill, and my face was still red and warm from our lovemaking. As we got nearer to the house, Percy let go of my hand and told me to go first up the drive to the house and then he would follow shortly after just in case the master was to see us.

"I lay in my small bed that night, a smile on my face for the first time in months. I felt happy, so happy that I could even put up with the head cook bullying me. I drifted off to sleep imagining our future together. I was content.

"In the kitchen the next morning, I was buttering my master's bread, ready to go alongside his smoked kippers. The silver tray was already waiting when Cook rang the service bell for the maid to come fetch the tray to take upstairs. The maid was called Isabel, a very pretty girl around seventeen, chubby-faced and a little plump. She had rosy red cheeks and curly ginger hair. Cook was saying how happy she looked this morning, a proper spring in her step. This made Isabel smile and touch her hair under her white cap. Isabel was showing Cook a ring on her left hand. Cook's hands clamped to her mouth, and she let out an excited squeal of delight. Isabel had got engaged. Cook and the other kitchen maid were hugging Isabel and spinning her around the kitchen. Cook was saying to her, 'You and Percy will be so happy together, a perfect pair.'

"That was the morning my whole world fell apart. The most ice-cold wave went all over my body, a wave that made me shake and feel sick. Sick to my belly.

"I had arranged to meet Percy again that night and had thought about having it out with him. I decided to keep what I had learned to myself and to try to make him want me as much as I wanted him. To put all thoughts of Isabel out of his mind.

"I let him enter me again and kiss my face and breasts. We sat hand in hand afterwards in silence, looking at the still of the river. I was staring at the reeds at the edge of the bank with a mixture of tears and rage coursing through me. I had to stop this impending wedding at all costs. I would do anything. The next morning the talk was of this darn wedding. Her father was going to give her away in the village church and then our master had generously said that the bridal party could have the use of one of the grand rooms for the reception where a simple spread would be available. It was his gift to both for their service to him and his wife.

"By now I was seething. I could feel my blood at boiling point. I had arranged again to meet Percy at the riverside later that evening. I waited and I waited, but he never came. I was devastated and extremely angry. I could not stop the tears. I thought how he had spoiled me. Made me his. How horrible Cook was to me. How I felt different and hated by everybody. I was better off dead. I walked down the sandy bank, partly on my bottom with my arm supporting me, as I could not see a thing through my hot and angry tears. I sat in the freezing water, grabbing handful after handful of mud, screaming loudly I was so distraught. I slithered further down the embankment until my white dress was drenched and heavy, the full skirt bellowing out with air and water. I could not catch my breath as the water hit me. I did not care. I inhaled the water repeatedly. Filling my lungs until they burned. I wanted this unbearable misery to end."

"Come with me this minute, girl. You have had enough time reading with that lost cause," Hairy Mole shouts at me, making me jump back into reality. "I need you to assist me with one of the lunatics." I duly follow her, wondering what cruel act will need my help. I soon find out. I am to be shown my first tube feeding of an unwilling patient. "This one has refused to eat for days. And now we need to force her with the aid of this." She shows me a long rubber tube. I feel horrified as this uncaring attendant is explaining what will happen. The patient is already restrained in the form of a strait dress – I call it a dress as it covers this woman's body and not just the top half, as a straitjacket would normally do. I am being told to hold the woman's head perfectly still. I am looking into the eyes of a terrified middle-aged woman, bulging with fear, wild-looking as if the devil himself is stood before her. Now she is making a dreadful inhuman growling noise, coming from deep within her throat, shaking her head violently from side to side.

"Hold it still, girl," another attendant orders me, pointing at the patient's head.

Hairy Mole, exasperated, says to this woman, "Keep still and do not struggle. It will be much worse if you fight against us."

The nasal tube is being prepared; it looks like rubber. The tube is being fed without much care through her nose now. One of the attendants is letting Hairy Mole know that it has successfully passed down the nasal cavity. The tube is now passing down her throat, which makes this wretch want to vomit, gag, and shake. She must feel as though she is suffocating as she is really struggling now, arching her back and trying to stand up. Even with the three of us restraining her, it takes all our strength to hold her writhing body. Once the feeding tube reaches her stomach, the patient calms down briefly. I say kindly to her to look at me and to concentrate on her breathing. Reassuring her that it will soon all be over. This does not go down at all well with

Hairy Mole as she snaps, "Don't mollycoddle them. It's her own fault it has come to this. Shut it and do what I tell you to do." My eyes fill with tears once again. My head is still down, looking into this woman's eyes. A tear drips off my nose onto the restraint of the white dress, its wetness spreading over the material.

Next a jug full of a greyish liquid is poured down this tube. The senior attendant is doing this too quickly as the gloopy mixture is threatening to spill over the funnel from which it is being poured into.

It is over now; the tube is removed from her stomach, and the woman is helped half-heartedly to sit up. She is saying she feels sick, and her stomach is fit for bursting. The answer to this problem is "Keep it down and don't sick it back, or we will have to start all over again."

Another voice barks another order. "Stop your complaining and be grateful we didn't let you starve to death." I am conscious now just how much I hate this prison of a place and how maybe the workhouse would serve these poor outcasts more favourably.

I am now placed on a small table next to Beady Eye. It is dark with just the glow of Beady Eye's oil lamp and my small lantern. It is nighttime. The dormitory is still, apart from a couple of the patients talking to themselves. I am sat at the entrance to the long dark ward. We have a sickness in the asylum, two extremely ill women that will need watching overnight. "Checks," Beady Eye orders me. I take my lantern and slowly make my way down the ward. The two poorly ladies are positioned near our desks so we can watch them more closely.

I am halfway down the dormitory now, silently moving so as not to wake them. Gertie is happily whispering away to an imaginary woman called Dorothy. I can hear her more clearly the nearer I get to her bed. She is talking about a wedding and how much she has missed Dorothy, laughing softly at Dorothy's reply that only Gertie can hear. She lifts her arms outstretched in front of her as if she is going to embrace this invisible lady. I shudder, partly with cold and partly with fear as I am wondering to myself that just maybe Dorothy's ghost is in the room. Moving along the ward, I check the other women one by one, shining my lantern over their faces. I am right at the far end now and all is well. I turn to go back to my station, but as I am turning around, I notice the big round clock positioned on the wall over our tables. I can see it is 3am, the time illuminated by Beady Eye's oil lamp. I look below the clock, and she is staring at me, the strict, uncaring face, looking harsh even in the soft glow of the lantern.

I am sat beside this mean attendant again now, and we notice that the poorly woman is getting worse, struggling with her breathing. I recognise the sound well, the death rattle. We both go over to her and discover she is wet with urine, not soaked through, just her nightgown and the rags beneath her. She has not been able to drink without choking for a day or two now. I am being sent by Beady Eye to the laundry room to fetch clean sheets and fresh rags to place between the patient's legs. We now roll her over to change the bottom sheet. Beady Eye has her oil lamp to the woman's bottom and is saying that this lady has a large open bed sore just between the top of her bottom and the base of her spine. I am to fetch a tub of linseed, and we rub into and around the wound. The patient groans slightly but mainly seems unaware of what we are doing. The poor patient is skin and bone, her eyes slightly open with a glazed look. Her skin is grey and waxy. Her cheeks are sunken. Lips dry and chapped. The look of death.

We clean her and make her comfortable on an extra pillow. "She has not got long for this world now. Poor soul," Beady Eye is saying as she reaches down and strokes this dying patient's hair. I feel astounded as this is the first act of kindness that this usually horrible attendant has ever shown. She must be sensing my bewilderment as she

99

follows the sentiment with "She is one of us. And a darn good nurse she was too."

"She worked here," I manage to say.

"She did indeed. From the age of eighteen right up until three years ago. She then developed a congestion of the brain and went quite mad. She must be eighty now." So that is why Beady Eye showed a bit of care. It all makes sense now. Before long, the death rattle passes and is quickly replaced by Cheyne-Stoking, something that shows death is only hours away. At 6am the elderly lady passes away peacefully with Beady Eye holding her hand. I am sure I see her wiping a single tear from her face.

We are both on night duty again tonight, almost twenty-four hours later. The same procedure occurs as the night before. I am doing my checks with the soft glow of my lantern, passing Gertie, who is happily playing imaginary catch with her ghost, Dorothy. Others are sleeping soundly. Others staring into nothingness. I make my way back to our station. My eyes are feeling heavy, the ticking of the clock soothing me.

"Wake up, girl. No use to me sleeping on the job."

I feel a sharp jab in my arm. "Sorry," I say, still half asleep.

The other lady who is gravely ill is struggling and looks uncomfortable, moaning and groaning as if in pain. The doctor visited this middle-aged lady earlier in the day and recommended the day attendants make a mustard poultice to try and ease the patient's aches and pains.

On my next checks, I looked for the plaster but cannot find it. I gently slide my hand underneath her bottom. She is wet with urine, and by the feel of her, she has not been changed in a long time. I ask Beady Eye for help. I have already gone to the laundry for fresh linen and rags. Beady Eye sighs and ambles over to the bed, grumbling that what is the point in changing her as she "Hasn't got long." Her attitude is different from that of the previous night. As I roll this frail, fragile woman towards me, a small amount of blood trickles from the corner of her mouth. I take a clean rag and wipe it away, thinking Beady Eye will be shocked or at least show concern. "It's the drink that's done that to her. Her insides are rotting," is her brisk reply, followed by, "She was a woman of ill repute, going to most of the local drinking houses, guzzling as much stout as she could get into her. No money, of course. The men folk would pour the drink down her in return for immoral favours."

I feel shock and pity for this poor woman, wondering what drove her to this behaviour. I don't need to wait long to find out. "Her husband could not do a thing with her. She accused him of beating her regularly. All nonsense, of course. He is a lovely man."

I am feeling brave and intrigued, so ask, "Why is she here?"

The answer is frank. "She caught a disease from all the men. Syphilis, comeuppance for her sins. Filthy loose woman. It addled her brain, joints, liver. Everything. Her innards are rotten through. She became uncontrollable. Her husband could not control her violent outbursts so had her committed to us."

How sad, I thinking inwardly. "What could have been done for her?" I dare to ask.

This question is met with a sarcastic laugh, followed by, "The doctor tried everything to cure her. She had the lot. Cold-water shock treatment. Purging treatment. The last resort was small doses of arsenic. Nothing worked, so she spent two years in the padded rooms in isolation before she became like this. God's will, it is. She must repent. This is God's will."

Not long after the familiar sound of Cheyne-Stoking appears. The blood is still oozing from her mouth, forming little bubbles that gently pop before the next one appears. The poor dear hangs on for another four days before her body and soul finally find peace. I am sad for this lady. So sad.

I crawl into my hard, uncomfortable bed, crying like I have never sobbed before. Crying for my mother. My father. My brothers. These poor lost souls. Everything. I am feeling like I have a hard round ball in my throat, slowly squeezing the last drops of tears out of me. I fall into a fretful sleep full of all my worst nightmares.

The empty beds are soon filled with two more hapless patients. Awaiting their fate and cruel, derogatory treatment to cure them. Free them of their madness.

I am now going down a long corridor. I recognise from the dank smell of damp where I am going. I am looking for Esme. She didn't showed up for breakfast and I missed her first thing as Gertie had wet the bed again. I soon find her walking aimlessly, talking to herself. "They are all trying to poison me. They want me dead to quieten me. So my lips shall not ever tell." Esme is shaking and acting erratically.

"Esme, you must try to compose yourself. If the other attendants see you like this, they will be sure to tell Matron and the doctor. You will be sent back to the padded room. Now I know that you don't want that. Do you?" I try to reason gently.

"But they want me dead. Dead, I tell you. Everyone I know wants me to be dead. My family and especially Percy and that bitch he is to marry."

I am rubbing Esme's back now, as if comforting a distressed infant. "Esme. I am listening to you, and I will try and help you. Remember the reading sessions? If you continue like this, then that will stop, and you will be taken away again. Do you understand?" I am doubtful she does as she is fiddling with a piece of cloth that she has found, twiddling it around and around her fingers, only stopping to pull at her hair.

I have a thought. "Esme. Gertie must be missing you at breakfast. Shall we find her?" It works. Esme dutifully follows me to the confectionary where she takes her seat next to Gertie. I am watching them anxiously, hardly daring to breathe.

Gertie has her arms outstretched, saying, "My darling girl. My beautiful darling girl," stroking Esme's face like it is made of fine China, in much the same way a child would stroke a tiny fragile kitten. I watch some more to see that Esme is doing her usual in helping Gertie to eat, spooning the gruel into the hungry, gaping mouth. The patients have a treat this morning. A bread roll. Gertie has not a tooth in her head, and I notice that Esme has the presence of mind to soak it in Gertie's gruel to soften it. Gertie must have gums of steel though as she manages to chew through the gristly grey mutton. It's this simple act of kindness from Esme though that is warming my heart. Is this the act of a cold, callous lunatic? Esme takes a moment to wipe the dribble from Gertie's chin before looking over at me, smiling that beautiful warm, caring smile.

"Are you ready to come and read to me, Esme?" I ask, on tenterhooks.

"Yes, miss. I am ready."

"What happens when you have inhaled all of that muddy water?" I am trying to tread carefully with Esme due to her fragile state of mind earlier. I listen anxiously now as she explains that night's turn of events. She is now telling me freely.

"My lungs are clogging with thick stagnant mud. I can taste the grit. I do not care, just keep on breathing it in, gulping it down, waiting for death. For peace from this rage and desperation. I feel death near but am not afraid. I am in a misty tunnel of bright white. I open my eyes wide, watching the last air bubbles of my breath floating to the surface. I then see nothing but black, jet black. A blackness I have never seen before, followed by a prism of colours like a hundred rainbows. I feel total utter peace. A warm, comforting feeling spreading throughout my entire body. I am going faster and faster towards this promised peace, encouraging it to engulf me.

"Then as quick as that feeling happened upon me, it went. Just like that. Vanished. I was then being pulled back at such a speed that my hair and heavy dress rushed past my head. Next, I was back on the sandy bank of the river. I was hardly breathing, if at all. I was still not back in this world, but I felt in a sort of limbo between the two. Next my chest was being hit with what felt like a hammer, thumping down on my ribs repeatedly. Then I was being turned over and my back was being pummelled harder and harder until I vomited. I was sick. So sick. Thick, slimy, gritty mud was pouring from my mouth. Just when it was over, rough fingers were reaching down my throat, as far back as possible. I was now purging thicker black slime. My stomach would be next out of my mouth; I was certain of it.

"I then turned and saw the face who brought me back from somewhere I desperately wanted to go. A village woman coming back from her day peddling her goods at a market in the next town. A lady we knew locally as Loony Leonora. She lived in a ramshackle cottage deep within the woods. She was speaking to me softly, telling me I would be all right. I did not want to be all right; I wanted to be dead. And she had spoiled my plan. Ruined it. She loaded me on the back of her old cart, and making a clicking sound with her tongue to gee up her horse, we were off.

"She eased me off the cart and led me by my hand into this old fairytale cottage. I was laid down on a bed with an eiderdown covering me. I was given some sort of linctus and then she lit a bundle of what she called misty charcoal under my nose, reassuring me it would clear and soak up any impurities that were still in my body. I slept then. Slept like I had never slept before.

"When I awoke the next morning, I was aware of a tabby cat asleep at the foot of my bed. I sat up slowly and began to stroke the cat's soft fur. The cat started purring and kneading the bed clothes. Over by the window I noticed a bird in a cage with its wing bound up and strapped to its body. It looked like a young jackdaw with a smooth grey head. Everywhere I looked I saw plants and row upon row of small brown bottles with corks in the top.

"Next Leonora fed me some concoction. I didn't know what it was, and I did not ask. Soup then followed at dinner time, a thick rich soup that tasted wonderful. Every spoonful I ingested, I felt it doing me good. I spent the next few days with Loony Leonora and decided that she was not at all loony, just a solitary wise woman that wanted to live off the land and be surrounded by nature. Leonora took me back home to my mother, reassuring me that all would be well after we had told my mother what had happened.

"I was myself again for a week or two, then a black coat enveloped me once more along with the red mist of betrayal. Mother sent for the doctor, who prescribed an opium-based elixir called Kendal Black Drop. It sent me spiralling into a frantic, wild state and whatever this cure was, I am certain it was a poison to keep me from telling of my plight. I ran around to all my neighbours, hoping for solace. Protection. They offered nothing but tea, which I know had that awful elixir in it. They were all in it together. Mother, the doctor. The neighbours. Percy and that bitch. All of them making out I was mad. Mother could not cope with me. She did try by locking me in my room, but I just broke out or jumped out of the window. I was on a rampage to find out why I had been deceived and I was determined to find out, no matter the cost. The cost came sooner than I thought. Two policemen came to my mother's door along with a stern-faced woman. They took me, kicking and screaming, to the workhouse. They soon realised I was uncontrollable, thus I ended up here. I am not mad. Not crazy and not a lunatic."

As I end the reading session and Esme stands up and smooths her dress, I notice that her belly looks slightly swollen. Could it be malnutrition? Or something else?

"Come back, May. Three, two, one, come back. You are safe, back in the present day. You are back. Open your eyes slowly." Handing me a drink of water, Mark asked me softly if I was feeling OK.

"Yes, I am feeling perfectly well, Mark. I am finally getting somewhere with Esme."

"You are. You are indeed, May."

Chapter 16

1995

As I walked into work that Monday morning, I could not help but notice the design of my workplace, how the architects had kept the factory in its original form. Even the road leading up to the factory had kept its original cobbled entrance with the double iron gates now in full view as I turned the corner. To anyone living on the housing complex, you would be hard pushed to see it. I was pleased that they had kept this part. An important part of history like this shouldn't be buried and forgotten about like the poor lost souls that once lived and died behind these walls.

The factory had a different feel this morning. As I walked along the short corridor with its glaring florescent lighting above, I could almost feel arms clawing out of the walls, each one trying to grab at me as I passed. The white walls were replaced by the old thick stone walls, crying their tears once more. I shook my head to bring myself back.

"Morning, May," Maggie chirped, a little more chipper than normal.

"Hi, Maggie. You OK?" I enquired.

"I am splendid, May. I will be even better come the end of the week."

Of course! The end of the week signalled not only the impending Christmas party but also pay day, with the hope of the long-awaited bonus. Maggie and Sandra would be very disappointed if that didn't come into fruition, what with them both doing days of hard graft the previous week.

"Nancy. Good morning. And how are you this fine morning?" Maggie was pushing her luck now.

"I would be fine if it wasn't for this place. It is enough to drive me around the bend."

I laughed and said to Nancy, "Well, I haven't heard that expression for years. My nan would always say it when us kids were getting too noisy or getting under her feet."

I was still smiling to myself as Nancy replied, "Yes, my grandmother used to say it to us all the time. Difference being she knew all about being driven around the bend."

"Oh. How come, Nancy?" I often wondered where this old saying originated from. "This place. And others like it," Nancy said sternly, followed by, "All lunatic asylums were built with a long road leading up to the asylum, usually then followed by a large bend in the drive before you finally came to the asylum. Hence where the saying came from. Being driven around the bend."

I understood now. Never would I have put two and two together though. Nancy went on to explain that this was to try and stop local folk and some visiting folk from gawping at the spectacles that were these mad patients.

"Was your grandmother a patient at the asylum then, Nancy? As you said that your grandmother knew for real what being driven around the bend was like?"

"No, she worked here for years as one of the attendants on the female ward, right up until she married and had my mother."

So, the rumours I had heard about Nancy being involved in some way with the history of the asylum was true. "I imagine she had a lot of stories to tell you and your mother, Nancy?" I pushed her to tell me more.

"Nope. Not a thing. She was a nasty, bitter woman who had not one ounce of love in her." I could see the mere mention of her grandmother was evoking some unwelcome memories. Her shoulders had gone tight and moved up towards her ears. Nancy had a faraway look in her eyes. I knew not to push my luck any further. At least not today anyway.

"Bloody hell, May, you sure know how to put a damper on the day, don't you?" Maggie had managed to stay quiet up until this point.

"I was only asking out of interest. How was I to know that would be her reaction?"

Heading on into the factory, things were looking very festive indeed. Some red, blue, and gold tinsel hung from each of our biscuit-spewing machines. A Christmas tree was positioned just inside the factory door so that everyone on the factory floor could see it. Not that any of us had chance to admire the twinkling fairy lights, baubles, and more tinsel that had been thrown on as if it was an afterthought. If I looked up for even a second, I would be in trouble. Biscuits do not stop coming for no one. The local radio was on and was playing lots of carols and the latest pop group singing a Christmas song, in the hope that theirs would be number one, or at the very least in the top-ten countdown on the big day.

I glanced over quickly at the garibaldi bunch, as we called them. They packed those along with rich teas. They had Father Christmas hats on and even some fun festive earrings. Over the far right side was what we referred to as the plain janes, as they had the plain boring biscuits, digestives and malted milks. Finally, the last four of our little factory group we called the runners for obvious reasons as their sole job was the fig rolls. They also had the grand, honoured job of handling and taking all our packed biscuits out the front, ready for the delivery driver to collect and take to the various shops and supermarkets around the county.

As the week drew on, the excitement was building daily. Maggie and Sandra were reaching fever pitch. Inside our kitchenette was a cardboard box that had been painted red, a makeshift post box for the staff to post their cards through if they wished. This always created some sort of wager on who would be honoured to have the privilege each day of opening said box and putting the cards into neat little piles. I wasn't bothered about not being picked, but some of the staff took it seriously, Maggie and Sandra being the two most competitive. I think, looking back, it was just an excuse to have an extra five-minute break, a perk if you like. I just wanted to do my work and go home.

It was decided on the Thursday, before the grand event on the Saturday, that the four of us would meet at Sandra's house and have a few Babychams and a Cinzano or two. *I will be tipsy before I get to the party*, I thought to myself. Colin was looking about as pleased as I felt but agreed with the plan. We dared not do otherwise.

"I wish my girlfriend could come too," Colin simpered.

This of course left him open to shouts of "For goodness' sake, Colin, what's up with you? Live a little for God's sake."

Maggie loved to tease him, and as always Sandra would follow suit with, "Yes, Colin. You two aren't joined at the hip, you know." Colin couldn't say or do right for doing wrong.

Just before clocking off, I asked Nancy if she was looking forward to the meal and disco. "No, I am not," she briskly replied. I decided to leave it at that for now as she looked in no mood to talk.

"Nancy seems extra fed up today and is not looking forward to the Christmas do," I said to my three workmates.

"Ah well, that is up to her, ain't it? Bloody miserable cow." Maggie was not bothered at all about Nancy or why she did not feel excited about the meal. Whilst I knew that feeling well, I found it strange that Nancy seemed very anti-Christmas party. She must have been to so many after all the years she had worked here.

Sandra piped up, "Just you wait until she opens that whip and handcuffs, which will cheer her up no end. Wont it, Mags?" The screeching pair were uncontrollable again, holding onto each other they were laughing so much at the very thought of it.

"Oh, don't, Sandra. Stop it. I am going to pee myself," Maggie declared, hopping on one leg.

Colin looked either repulsed, sick, or even both! "Come on, Colin, let us leave the giggling Gerties to it. We have homes to go to." It was nice to walk out with someone as usually I would finish early on the weekdays and walk alone. Steve had broken up early for the holidays, so he was going to fetch the children from school, which of course they loved. A nice novelty for Millie and Toby and for Steve too. Plus, it meant that I could work another couple of hours, which would really help what with Christmas just around the corner.

"What is your plan for next year, Colin? Any New Year's resolutions on the cards?" I asked as we huddled in our big winter coats, trying to stay warm. It was another typically cold December evening. The freezing fog had set in for the night, and you could see the icy mist it was forming against the orange light of the streetlamps.

"I have no idea, May, but one thing is certain: I am going to be leaving the factory once I have found another job. I cannot stick it there much longer."

I was sad to hear that Colin wanted to leave and expressed the fact along with, "Is it because of Maggie and Sandra always pulling your leg?"

"No, not that, May. I know they mean me no malice and it is all done in jest, even if it is at my expense. No, I am just wanting more in life than packing biscuits. I want to train to be a paramedic." Colin would make a great paramedic, very calm and steady. He wouldn't panic or lose his temper. He would be ideal.

After saying our goodbyes and "See you in the morning," I was soon at home, the heat of the radiators giving me a warm welcome as I came in. Millie and Toby came rushing through from the living room to greet me, kissing my cheek and hugging me.

"Daddy picked us up from school today, Mummy."

Which of course I knew as I had been the one to arrange it, but still I went along with the excitement and replied, "How lovely, you are a lucky pair. I bet you loved having Daddy pick you up. You must have been so pleased to see him."

They could not get their answers out of their mouths quick enough as they both said in unison, "Yes, we were pleased to see Daddy. And so was Lucinda. She hugged Daddy and said how nice it was to see him again."

I bet she did, I thought to myself scathingly, but instead replied, "Ah, that was nice of her."

Steve came through from the kitchen. "All right then, love. Thought I would go to the chippy tonight. Treat us all as its Christmas."

"Yes, lovely, Steve. Just the job." I sniffed the air in front of Steve, taking in overexaggerated breaths. "Is that Chanel No 5 I can smell?" I asked.

"What's that when it's at home?" Steve looked genuinely confused.

"I will put it in simple terms for you, Steve. Lucinda!" I teased half-heartedly.

"What you on about now, May?"

I tried not to give it away by smiling too much. I was going to enjoy winding Steve up for as long as I could. "Give you a little clue, Steve. Red lippy, long legs up to her armpits, long blonde hair, perfect figure, and gorgeous-looking." The penny was being terribly slow to drop, unless Steve was playing clever, as whatever answer he gave he might be in trouble. "Lucinda. Cuddle. Nice to see you again!" I had spelt it out now.

"Oh, that Lucinda. Yes, she bound up to me and gave me a lovely greeting." The penny had now dropped.

"You make her sound like a golden retriever, Steve." I could not hide my giggles anymore. "I am winding you up. Don't look so worried."

Steve laughed and looked relieved at the same time. "I knew you were, love. Anyway, there is only room for one woman in my life and she is standing right in front of me."

Forever my mister smooth. I laughed, then hugged him. "Come here, you soft sod." We were always winding each other up, neither of us knowing until the last minute if we were being serious or not. We were very well practised at it by now.

Still hugging, Steve kissed the top of my head, saying, "Cod and chips is it, love?"

Cod and chips and seeing Mark later. This was turning out to be a good day. A very good day indeed.

Chapter 17

1845

I am being told early one morning that it is time to bath Esme, not a cold-water therapy bath but an ordinary warm bath. It is nearing Christmas and all of us attendants have been told the same by the senior nurses. I am led to believe that some of the patients might have a visitor over the festive season, so the authorities need to make sure they are all well-kept and in the best possible condition. Hair washed, finger and toenails trimmed, and teeth cleaned. The irony is that not one of the patients are to have a visitor and the senior nurses, matron, and the superintendents know as much. They don't want to risk being exposed, though, should an unexpected relative crawl out of the woodwork. For most of the patients, Christmas Day will be much the same as any other day in the asylum.

Nevertheless, I coax Esme into the cold, sparse bathroom. I can tell she is not keen on this idea of a bath as the only meeting that she has had so far with water has not been a good experience at all. Esme has built up trust with me over the last three weeks that I have been her attendant, but even so I can see her visibly shaking and not just due to the cold bathroom. I allow her now to feel the water to reassure her that it is warm and not ice-cold. Esme very wearily dips her fingers into the water, swishing them around until she is satisfied that I am not lying to her. I now very gently help to take off her long, dirty off-white nightgown. Esme clings on to me for support as I encourage her into the bath water.

Once I have settled her into the large tub, which sits in the middle of the room, with two other baths each side, I leave a bar of carbolic soap on the side so that she can wash herself, explaining that I will leave her to have some privacy whilst I make her bed and sort out a fresh bundle of clothes for her. Esme is very calm and understanding of the fact that I will not leave her long. I am rushing now, conscious that I must not go a minute over my time, as I fear that it might undo all the trust that we built up together.

As I enter the bathroom, I am relieved that Esme is still sat where I left her. "Right, Esme, the next thing I am going to do is give your hair a wash. You are quite safe, and you are not to be afraid. No harm will come to you, I promise." I slowly pour warm water over her long, matted hair, using a mixture made of olive and soda. The first lather does nothing, the second makes a few suds, so I will have to put this mixture on for a third time. The water is black, the blackest, dirtiest water I have ever seen aside from ditch water. Too dirty to wash the suds out. I head over to the large copper boiler and carefully scoop a ladle of warm water out of it. I have to go back to the boiler three more times until the water from her hair runs clean.

I am now holding a wide tooth comb, which looks like it is made from bone. Her hair is still so matted and knotted but clean at least. I gently tease it until all the knots are at the bottom of Esme's hair. I will need to cut around an inch off from the bottom of her hair to get them all out. Esme is compliant with this and allows me to do it free of fuss.

This only leaves the finger and toenails to be trimmed now. I decide to do this once I have helped Esme out of the bath, as by now the water is only slightly warm. The water has softened the nails with any luck, making them much easier to cut.

Now Esme is sat safely in a chair by the side of the bath, wrapped in a large rough and scratchy towel, the familiar grey colour standing out against the white of the bathtub. I have now cut her fingernails, which did not take long as Esme is a nail biter. Many of the other women are, I have noticed. Esme's toenails are a different matter altogether, though, so long that they have started to curl in on themselves and the nail on one of her big toes has started to grow inwards, the skin around the toe scarlet. It must be sore, but Esme doesn't complain as I go about cutting that one and the others that follow.

It is when Esme stands up that I am most shocked. She is skin and bone. Poor mite. Shoulder blades jutting out like angel wings were starting to grow. Her shoulders look like they belong to someone else entirely. They are swollen, and the bones look too big for her small frame. Her knees are similar, oversized and misshapen. I am now thinking, could it be rickets? Or is she just so painfully thin that her bones look too big for her tiny frail body?

Esme has her back to me, still standing up, and I notice now that her hair is drying. It has a slight wave in it and is the most beautiful dark auburn colour, as opposed to the dirty brown it was before. I walk towards Esme, just as she is turning around to face me, still naked. I gasp now, putting my hands over my mouth in shock. I had noticed days before that Esme's belly looked a little swollen, but now I am seeing her bare in the cold light of day, her belly isn't just a little swollen but positively rounded. I am still hoping that is through a poor diet and not the other reason that is floating in my mind.

I now have to tread very carefully with Esme so as not to scare or unnerve her. Her mind is still extremely fragile. Once Esme is in her fresh bundle of clothes, I very casually ask her when she last had her curse. "I do not have them anymore, miss. Not since they poisoned me, horrible hags." I ask if she can remember when her last curse had come upon her. "It was when I was a scullery maid, miss. My last one happened just before I met that pig." Now that the memory is fresh in her mind, Esme is blaspheming again, calling Percy and the kitchen maid every name under the sun, swearing, spitting venom like an angry snake, pulling at her hair as if in despair. She says she would kill them given the chance. I am leaving it for now, I decide. I shall watch the belly to see if it gets bigger. Then I will know whether this poor mite is with child. If she is with child, she will not fare well in here.

Christmas morning has arrived, and I feel the least festive I have ever felt, thinking of my home and family more than ever this day. We did not have very much. Mother spending all of Christmas Eve preparing the food was one of my most favourite times. I remember with both fondness and sadness as in my mind's eye I see Mother rolling out the pastry for the mince pies, then cutting it into circles, ready for me to fill the cases. I first grease the tins with lard, then I put the larger pastry circles into the hollowed-out tins, spooning the mincemeat that Mother has so lovingly made, and adding a good glug of brandy, of course. Then finally after I have wetted the edge with egg, I press the smaller lid on, brush with more of the beaten egg, and prick a little hole into the top of each one. They then go into the range, which the fire is keeping red-hot. I am only about six and I stand by the range, willing the pies to cook quickly. The smell was unbelievable, hot pastry, spice, and brandy. I can feel my mouth watering even now, imagining them hot out of the range, cooling on an old iron cooling rack. I am sure my brothers and my father could smell them from across the fields, as Mother was always ready for them as they rushed into the kitchen, grabbing one each as they ran past. Mother would whack them playfully with a tea towel. "Get off, you rascals."

Next on my mother's list of jobs was making the stuffing all from scratch, peeling the vegetables and standing them in cold water ready for the grand day. The Christmas cake had been made three moths beforehand, being lovingly fed regularly with either brandy or the homemade sloe gin. Mother would ice the Christmas cake two weeks before Christmas so the icing was lovely and hard. My job was to decorate it with a little robin and a donkey, all finished off with a bright red bow.

I am now in the small front room with my brothers. The excitement I feel is the most wonderful feeling, like I could burst. My brothers would have a small wooden car each that our father had lovingly made for them, Usually one was painted blue, the other one red. My present was a small wooden dolly made from one of my mother's large wooden pegs, along with a small carved puppy which father had made, sheep's wool for my doll's hair and straw for the puppy's fur. My kind, thoughtful mother had even knitted a tiny little dress for my dolly. The last treat was to be found at the very bottom of the pillowcase, an orange and some of Mother's wonderful homemade sticky sweet fudge.

I am now back in the women's dormitory, and they are all being herded like cattle towards the large, freezing cold bathroom. Stood in line one behind the other, waiting to have their wash. The patients that can wash themselves have a very quick wash, face, under arms, and their tuppence. Those women that cannot or will not wash themselves just stand at the sink looking into the basin for two minutes or so. They must be so conditioned just to follow the crowd and more than likely have no idea what they are supposed to be doing.

As it is Christmas Day, not many other attendants are on duty. They try to take it in turns each year to have part of the day off. There is no way that the young attendant and I could help forty women have a wash.

Gertie is wondering about the bathroom, soaking wet with urine as usual. I must wash her as she has that familiar ammonia smell again. Coaxing her to the sink, I give her a quick wash with a carbolic soap that is still hanging around. "Come on, Gertie. It is an incredibly special day today, you know."

Gertie has no idea that it is Christmas morning. "Is it, dear?" is her only response.

Next, we all head to the dining area where instead of the usual gruel the patients are served one piece of bread, spread with the smallest amount of fat that you can hardly see, along with the warm, milky sweet tea.

The young attendant who tells me her name is Tess is very pleasant and speaks to me kindly. What a treat to have Tess working alongside me. I feel I could hug her for being so nice, totally different from Hairy Mole and Beady Eye, whom we are told are starting their shift at dinner time.

Next, once breakfast is over with, we take the ladies into the dayroom as usual. The piano is open with a nurse sat expectantly on the stool, ready to play. I am being told by Tess that this nurse has come down from one of the other wards to play for us all. "Wonderful." I smile. Once the women are more settled, the nurse begins to play, firstly some lovely calming music. I do not know what it is, but it sounds classical. Next a candle is lit that sits on the top of the piano. This at once catches the more sensible patients' attention. We are being waved over by the nurse to gather around the piano. The women are excited now as Christmas carols are starting to be played, one after the other. Some of us know the words, some do not. We all come together as one group, and it does not matter that not all the words are known; they are all smiling and that is giving me the warmest feeling. One of the younger patients leads Gertie by the hand and starts to dance with her, twirling this way and that. Gertie is beaming, saying, "Darling girl. This is so much fun." Before long we all take a partner and dance, even ones that have not got a partner to pair up with, for Tess and myself are dancing with three or four at time. My head is thrown back as I am spinning around and around.

I am now suddenly standing stock still. I can hear laughter, shrieks of laughter. I look around the room and realise it is coming from me. Yes, me. I cannot quite believe it. I have not heard my own laughter since I have been in this place. I am looking around me again and every single woman is dancing along to the music. Free once more. Sane once more. Happy once more. I am feeling the tears run down my face, not tears of the familiar sadness though, but tears of pure genuine happiness.

Tess grabs me and twirls me around. "Merry Christmas, May." She laughs loudly.

"Merry Christmas, Tess," I reply, wiping my eyes.

We are all happy and having a wonderful time. Once the nurse has finished playing and has left to go back to her duties, we play some simple easy games. Some of the women are tired out from all the dancing and excitement so choose to sit and doze in the chairs or sit happily watching the others play.

I can hear a rattling now and the doors open into the dayroom. An old wooden trolley is being wheeled in by one of the kitchen staff, and upon the trolley is some cups and two big jugs with what looks like freshly squeezed orange juice in them. Closely following behind is the matron and two senior superintendents. They are smiling, going around each patient in turn, wishing them a "Merry Christmas," and handing them a piece of fruit. All the women are incredibly pleased, and those that can thank them and return the "Merry Christmas."

I am blinking now, thinking that I am in a dream. Never have I ever seen kindness of this degree shown to the women. Tess, sensing my bewilderment, leans over and explains that the local community always donates fruit for the patients every year. "A sort of tradition, I think," Tess says. I help to cut up the fruit for those patients that have no teeth or simply do not know what to do with it.

Dinner time soon rolls around. A big loud bell is being rung and the dayroom door swings open once more. "Ten minutes until dinner," a tall stately man in a very dapper suit is saying. As the door closes again, I can smell the wonderful aroma of a proper roast dinner, as opposed to the normal boiled cabbage.

"Time for the toileting run," both Tess and I say, only this time I almost have a spring in my step.

Now all the women that need help have been toileted, we head into a huge ballroom, a room that I have never been in before. A big, decorated Christmas tree stands in the corner of the room. Tables in long rows have been set, along with some greenery as a centrepiece on each. The dinner is delicious. Roast turkey with all the trimmings, followed by Christmas pudding. Tess and I enjoy a plateful along with our patients. We are both so full, as if we might burst, but we make sure we eat every single scrap.

Now I am folding something into my napkin, a piece of Christmas pudding. I will save that for later. The ballroom is full, and for once I am feeling warm. The male wing has joined us, along with their attendants. It has been a long time since I have seen any men, and I observe them all. They are acting in much the same way as our women, trying to wander around, playing with their food, and some rocking back and forth. The last time I saw a man was my father, apart from the doctors here, of course, and judging by Tess's face, she has not seen too many men either! The way she is making eyes at one attendant is blatant. "Tess," I exclaim, and we both look at each other and giggle like a couple of giddy teenagers.

After the feast, there is more music and dancing. Both the male and female patients are dancing, all under strict supervision, of course. There is only one fly in the ointment, which is when Hairy Mole and Beady Eye make an appearance. They enter the room, adjusting their caps, ready for duty. Surprisingly though, even the two of them have a very slight smile on their faces. Beady Eye's face looks particularly red and ruddy, as if she has drunk a sherry or two.

The two superintendents and the matron are making their way around the room. They are at our table now, so both Tess and I stand up at once. I feel I should curtsy or something as the air they have about them is powerful. Wishing us Merry Christmas once more, one of the doctors whom I have not seen before asks, "Have you enjoyed the festivities so far?"

We are both struck dumb for a second, before I manage to say, "Yes, thank you, sir."

121

The young doctor who I do not recognise smiles a kind, genuine smile, which shows in his eyes as he replies, "Please call me Doctor Fallon." He holds out his right hand for me to shake, offering the same gesture to Tess. The doctor goes on to say that he is new here in this asylum and is very keen to see how things are done. Doctor Fallon then moves on to the next table.

"Well, I never," an excited Tess says. I, in turn, smile and give her a wink. Just maybe things are going to slowly change for the better, I pray silently to myself.

Shortly after the doctor's greeting, I notice Esme sat on her own, looking frightened and extremely anxious. Not wanting things to escalate, I gently ask, "What's wrong, Esme? You look worried."

Her reply makes my stomach lurch. "The poison is taking hold, miss, I just know it. Something is wriggling in my belly, feels like worms or butterflies crawling in my innards, miss."

Touching her shoulder, I ask, "When did you first notice this feeling, Esme?"

"Few days ago, miss. I dared not tell anyone case they thought my madness was back. It is getting stronger now, though, and I fear the poison has made my innards rotten like that gal down the ward, the one that pegged it with the blood and everything coming from her. It's me next, I know it. I'm done for."

I know it now for sure. Esme is with child. I need to help her.

"May. Three, two, one. You are now back in the safety of my room; the fire is comforting and warm. You are with me, safe."

"I am back with you, Mark, and fully aware. That poor mite is pregnant."

"I know. I was there with you, May."

Chapter 18

1995

We were all gathered at Sandra's house, getting ready for tonight's big event. Yep, the night had finally rolled around, and I for one could not wait to get it over with so my Christmas with my family could begin. Sandra and Maggie both had noticeably short, extremely low-cut black glittery dresses on. Their hair was plumped up and backcombed, no doubt kept in place by a ton of hairspray. They looked very nice indeed. I just hoped Maggie would not drop anything and bend over to pick it up. Poor old Mr Gaskill would never recover! Her bosoms really did look as though they may escape at any moment, and she would certainly have to be careful if she were to perform any overzealous dance moves.

I had treated myself and had my hair blow dried at the local salon, just to give it a bit of bounce and body. I had chosen a close-fitting burgundy dress with a sparkly neckline and a pair of black patent high heels. A bit of make-up and that was me done. Colin looked very smart in a plain black suit with a nice pale blue shirt, his black curly hair swept back with gel. Yes, we certainly made a handsome four and scrubbed up well.

Sandra popped open a bottle of Lambrini as we held out glasses to be filled with the sparkling fizz. "Cheers, girls, and Colin. Merry Christmas to you all." We clinked our glasses and returned the festive wishes back to Sandra.

"Right then, I reckon that we ought to have another snifter for the road. What do ya think?" Maggie was keen in making this suggestion.

"Just a small one for me, please," I tried to get out, but it fell on deaf ears, of course, as Maggie poured a large glass of Cinzano with only a dash of lemonade.

"Get it down you, girl, it will put hairs on ya chest," Maggie shrieked.

Colin was on his fourth Cinzano and seemed to be enjoying the warm feeling that the alcohol was giving him. He was laughing. Now that was a first.

"Go steady, Colin. Don't forget we have wine on the table and a couple of drinks each at the bar. Don't want you being sick everywhere."

"Give it a rest, May. What are you, his mother?" both Sandra and Maggie echoed.

I put my hands up in front of me and just said, "OK. Fill your boots, Colin."

Walking into the hotel foyer, a young lady took our coats, then directed us to our table. "Bloody hell, gals, this ain't half posh," was Maggie's first impression, closely followed by her partner in crime.

"It really is. Gawd, we better behave ourselves tonight."

If only I could bank on that sentiment, I thought inwardly. I had a strong feeling it was going to go either one of two ways: either they would be on their best behaviour and act quite the ladies or get drunk out of their minds. I felt if I was a betting person, it would be the latter. *Oh well, that's up to them*, I decided, taking a large swig of wine myself.

I wished my prawn cocktail would hurry up and come. I was feeling slightly tipsy already and needed food. Colin by now was looking very hazy-eyed and had a permanent grin fixed on his face. Looking around the room at all the other tables, I spotted Nancy sat with Mr Gaskill and his family. I supposed that Nancy would have to sit with them, being our supervisor. On the factory's last day, just before closing, we all exchanged our Secret Santa gifts. I really hoped that Nancy liked her earrings and wondered if she was wearing them this evening. I could see that Nancy had a black dress on, so I imagined they would go well with her outfit.

The food was wonderful and really did surpass our expectations. Next the DJ was getting ready to start. The disco ball started to turn on the ceiling and flashing lights of red, blue, and green were attached to both the speakers. The DJ was asking for dedications and for any pop songs we particularly wanted him to play. Maggie and Sandra nearly broke their necks trying to get past Colin and me. They were, of course, first on the dance floor. No surprise either that Maggie had asked for 'Gangsta's Paradise' by Coolio. Not wanting to be left out, Sandra's choice was 'Disco 2000' by Pulp. The DJ was excellent and managed to get all of us up dancing, even me and Nancy. He played all the old favourites, Wham, Madonna, and of course 'Fairytale of New York' by The Pogues. It was a fantastic night. We hardly sat down, and even Colin was up dancing with us all, swinging us about and singing along to Bon Jovi or doing the birdie song.

Slowly the night started to end with the usual array of smoochy slow songs. Maggie and Sandra were slow dancing together. I sat down with a heavy thump onto my chair. My feet were killing me from all the dancing. Taking my shoes off and rubbing my sore feet, I noticed Nancy coming over to our table and she sat down next to me.

"Are you all right, Nancy?" She looked a little preoccupied.

Nancy sighed and said, "No. Not really. My mother has just been put into the local nursing home." I could see this was very upsetting for Nancy and I did not know if it was the drink that had made her tell me this news or something else. I listened as Nancy went on to tell me that her mother was a hundred and one years old and had been so independent until lately. Nancy had tried to care for her at home, but it all became too much for her, what with working as well. The difficult decision was made to put the old lady into a nursing home, something that Nancy's mother did not want and she made that feeling known to all that would listen. "Now as a result Mother isn't speaking to me and is refusing to see me." I felt desperately sorry for Nancy and reasoned that her mother would come around given time. I went to the bar and brought Nancy a brandy. She certainly looked like she needed it.

Just as Nancy knocked it back in one go, Maggie and Sandra wobbled back over to the table. "Whoa, Nancy, you are getting some Dutch courage in ya before trying that whip and handcuffs out. You dark horse, you." They of course were hooting with laughter.

"Not now, you two. Not now." I glared at them.

"My mother does not like any form of institution whatsoever. Her own mother worked in a huge institution and loved it there. Once she married my grandfather, though, she had to leave, as back then married women were not allowed to work, either by their employee or their husband. When she fell pregnant with my mother, she resented both my grandfather and my mother in equal measures. As far as she was concerned, they had ruined her life and made her give up the job that she enjoyed so much. My grandmother treated my mother appallingly, no love, no care, and no joy. It got back to my mother that she treated her patients in much the same way."

"Patients?" I enquired. "Was she a nurse?"

Nancy made a clicking sound with her tongue touching the roof of her mouth. "No, she was an attendant in the old Victorian asylum."

My legs almost give way; my stomach went over in a somersault fashion. "Which asylum, Nancy?" I just had to ask.

"The one that was here, May, where part of it still remains. The factory."

I felt lightheaded for a minute, and it was not due to the drink. "She was a nasty, cruel, spiteful woman and put the fear of God in me. I can just remember her. I see her mean face in my nightmares still to this day. A craggy old bitter face bearing down on me. Closer and closer her face looms, until all I can see is that big fat hairy mole on her top lip."

We both shuddered simultaneously. Nancy went on to tell me that her own mother never showed any love or tenderness to her. "Just doing the bare essentials to keep me alive." She said that her mother was never cruel in the sense that she beat her or anything like that, but the missed love of a mother hit her hard and had affected her whole life. I found out that Nancy had never married or had children and lived alone as she did not know how to show love and did not want to inflict that feeling on anyone else.

"Drink was banned, the devil's blood. Makes a woman loose and immoral," Nancy was explaining in detail. Is that why she had got so drunk a few months ago on our night out? I could not help but wonder. I dared to asked Nancy what had become of her grandmother. "She died young, at home, peacefully in her sleep with my mother holding her hand. She had nursed her throughout her short illness. Unbelievable really considering how she was treated herself growing up. That is conditioning for you."

How would I tell Nancy that I was almost certain that I had met her grandmother, the formidable Hairy Mole? I decided to keep this information to myself for the time being as I needed to know more about Hairy Mole to be certain it was her. I had a long time to wait, though, as Mark was on a Christmas break for two weeks. I had a feeling this time would drag.

Chapter 19

1846

The festivities are well and truly over. After the joyous day of Christmas is over, normal service resumes. Boxing Day is just the same as any other day, apart from a few slices of leftover cold ham and some dried-up turkey served at lunch along with bread and butter, washed down with the warm tea. After lunch it is decided that we are to take the patients on a walk around the vast grounds, much to Hairy Mole and Beady Eye's annoyance. We are instructed to gather the women into the large area known as the hall, where we are to find a box of shawls and hats for the women to put on.

"All this extra work for us. It's all wrong, you know," Beady Eye is moaning under her breath.

"Yes, it's all right for him sat in his warm room," Hairy Mole adds, in agreement.

I have discovered from Tess that all this is the new doctor's idea. Doctor Fallon is of the mind that fresh air is good for the mind and the body. I am thinking, could this one man alone help to ease the suffering of these women and have some power to create kindness and care? Could this be a small step in making things better? I hope so, with all my heart.

We all set off for our walk and a slight frost is still on the ground. Crows are cawing overhead, magpies squabbling for scraps of food that Cook has put out. I am inhaling this crispness of the chilly air, making my lungs go tight and taking my breath until I have acclimatised to it. There is a low watery sun shining, sending its feeble warmth down upon us, making the remnants of the frost sparkle like diamonds.

We walk a little further on down the pathway with Hairy Mole leading, Beady Eye at the rear of the group, and Tess and I floating up and down the middle. All the women are in pairs. We come across a pavilion with a group of about fifteen male patients and three attendants, some sitting on the wooden benches, some standing. All of them smoking. This is causing great excitement from both groups, the men cheering and shouting hello at us all. Our women are jumping up and down with delight at seeing the men again, grinning and waving. All apart from Gertie, who is happily talking to Dorothy still, showing her the few remaining dead leaves that are clinging to the trees. Esme is not taking any notice and is looking the other way.

Tess spots the male attendant she was flirting with on Christmas Day and dares to throw him a wave, which is promptly stopped by Beady Eye. Never one to miss anything, she bellows at Tess, "Stop that now, girl. You will end up a patient with such brazen behaviour."

We walk on further and come across about twenty women all chained together in what looks like a long cable, and each patient has a belt around their waist. The leader in front is a nurse, and the one behind is also a nurse. I recognise her as the pianist from Christmas Day. Four attendants are dodging in between, trying to keep order. Some of these women are shouting out and swearing, some trying to escape their shackles, one is holding her arms up towards the sky, preaching to the Lord himself. The quieter ones of the group are happily talking to themselves. Just behind this spectacle is another two nurses pushing two patients in a wooden chair on wheels. The two ladies are shouting, swearing, and wanting to kill everyone and everything in sight, eyes rolling back and their heads thrusting back and forth. I notice that they are both in straitjackets.

I look across at Tess and, as if reading my mind, she informs me quietly so that Beady Eye does not hear, "They are the mad ones, the violent ones. The lost causes that no treatment has ever helped. No cure. All together there are around sixty patients, so they must be brought out in groups of twenty or the nurses would never control all of them at once."

I have never seen such a sight. I glance over at Beady Eye, making sure that she will not hear my next question to Tess. Beady Eye is preoccupied with the last two women in the line. They keep bending down, trying to touch the grass with their fingers. One of the women is convinced that the glistening frost is a ring that she lost years ago. "Keep moving and shut up!" is Beady Eye's response.

I take my chance and ask Tess, "How do you know all of this? And how do you know it is what Doctor Fallon wants?"

With another quick look back, Tess whispers to me, "We will all be called in to his room, one by one. Your turn will be soon as I have not long had my meeting. He wants to know how and what we think of this place, the staff, the patients. The lot." It is making more sense to me now as I have heard a rumour that old Doctor Jones is retiring, and Doctor Fallon is to be his replacement. So, it must be true and not just a rumour. This is pure music to my ears. Tess continues to tell me as much as she can before she is caught and reprimanded.

I am now finding out that this new doctor wants improvements made within the asylum, both with the care and treatment of the patients and staff alike. His idea is to make it more like the privately owned asylums. These private asylums are very grand and have dedicated nurses, attendants, and doctors. They are also extremely expensive. The type of patients they care for are not unlike our own group of women. Some I have heard have lost their minds after giving birth. Others have become so melancholic that they want to die. Others, I am told, have reached the age when their curse stops and have become insane. Their husbands, at a loss, have had them declared insane and committed. Two of the private asylum patients had been declared insane and committed as they were scorned by a lover and went insane with rage. These women's families, along with the others, had money. Some were even put into the private asylum by their husbands. The poor wives had discovered that their husbands had taken a mistress and rather than cope with the fallout of their infidelity, they just wanted rid of their wives, so they would be put away, and their fury at their husband's betrayal could be put down to insanity. The husbands could be free to pursue more affairs or set up house with their mistresses, the wife long forgotten and left to rot. These people with plenty of money could afford the best care. They had their very own attendant, who would never leave their side. Reading with them or playing the piano, taking a stroll or just sitting by the open fire talking. A night nurse would be on duty all night and would come running at the first inkling of the ringing of a small bell that sat at the side of their beds. Only the best food was served, proper food three times a day with cups of tea and plates of cake aplenty.

I can't help but think to myself as I am laid in my small bed that night, how much an establishment like this would suit Esme. Alas, the thought is abruptly interrupted by the reason why Esme could never attend such a grand place. Money. Esme has nothing; her mother is a pauper. Poor Esme is trapped here in this godforsaken place like all of them.

The next morning arrives far too hastily, and I struggle to leave my semi-warm bed. I have had an unsettled night, thoughts of the previous day dwelling on my mind. I tossed and turned the best part of the night, the bottom sheet coming loose, making the cold oil cloth touch my body and chilling me to the bone.

I swill my face with water and have a quick wash. I am now in my uniform, heading to the dormitory. What I am faced with when I open the door is pure chaos. For there, laying on her bed, Esme is contorting as if the devil himself has possessed her, writhing her back, kicking legs, spitting obscenities, every swear word you can imagine. Amongst all this chaos is Hairy Mole, Beady Eye, and Tess, trying their best to keep Esme still and stop her from falling out of bed. I am now rushing over to Esme, and I take her hand, asking what the matter is, what has caused this upset. "The poison is working again, only stronger this time, miss. It is trying to get out of me, pushing my ribs out of the way so it can crawl out of my mouth."

Hairy Mole is huffing and puffing now, lifting Esme's nightgown to look at her bare belly. The sight that beholds us all is a white, round, bulbous stomach with what looks like something moving inside. Of course, now I am certain of what it is, and have been for a good while. Hairy Mole gasps and bellows to Tess, "Fetch for the matron, girl. Now hurry." Tess turns on her heels and runs as fast as she can out of the ward.

"What is it, miss? What is wrong with me?" Esme is looking at each of us in turn for an explanation. "Is it the poison? Is it the devil at work punishing me?" she pleads.

Hairy Mole looks her dead in the eye and responds, "Yes, you stupid girl. This is your punishment for your immoral actions. You are with child."

This means nothing to Esme, who I suspect has no clue about how a man plants his seed in a woman, and the consequence this can have. Poor, poor Esme. The worst has happened.

The doors to the dormitory fly open with vigour and a voice rages, "What the hell is going on?" This is not Matron.

"Matron wasn't about, miss, so I fetched Doctor Fallon." Tess is scrabbling to explain, knowing full well that both Hairy Mole and Beady Eye will not be pleased.

"Where is Matron?" Beady Eye wants to know.

"The matron is otherwise engaged. You have me instead. And I want to know this minute what all this commotion is about," Doctor Fallon answers her with authority and a no-nonsense approach. I think the pair of them have met their match and I am praying that I am next to be called into that room of his. This is my chance to let him know the full horror of this place.

The doctor calms Esme as much as he can, giving her a small amount of liquid in a galley pot. She is calm and sleeps for now. Doctor Fallon instructs me to stay and sit with Esme as she is holding my hand, saying, "Do not leave me, miss. Please do not leave me."

I am still sitting with Esme three hours later. Esme is starting to stir from her deep slumber, slowly opening her eyes and looking around the room as if getting her bearings. Suddenly she sits bolt upright, confused and very anxious, looking under the thin sheet that has been covering her. I take hold of her hand and gently reassure her as much as I can. "What is happening to me, miss? Am I ill? Am I dying?"

I now lay Esme back down, trying my best to calm her. I must put this to her as gently and calmly as possible, but most importantly I must be to the point in simple words that she will understand. "You are with child, dear Esme. Percy has planted a seed within you and now a baby is growing inside your stomach."

For a few minutes Esme is quiet and stares up at the high ceiling. "How has this happened to me, miss?" The innocence of this mite is frankly heartbreaking and quite shocking. I have to keep this extremely basic for Esme to fully understand. I am feeling a great responsibility now and wondering if I should leave it to the doctor to explain. I do not know this doctor well enough to be able to judge how he will break the news to her. Will he be blunt? Will he be brisk and uncaring and banish her again to the padded cells? No, I must be the one who explains. Esme trusts me.

I go on to explain that on one of the nights that she met with Percy, things went further than just kissing and fondling. Esme is looking intently at me and simply says, "Yes, miss. Things went further. I took me undergarments off, as did Percy. He told me that he was going to show me how much he loved me and how this next act would prove it. He was kind though, miss, told me it might sting a bit at first. Then we were united." Esme has no idea about such things and what can happen in these situations. "We did that about four times, miss, then I found out about that maid and the engagement."

As Esme is explaining this part to me, her face changes and the familiar look of rage replaces her innocence. I am both nervous and mindful when asking her to tell the next piece of the puzzle. I need to know every detail. For some reason I am compelled to know everything. "I was enraged, miss. The betrayal and the feeling of despair came about me. The copper kettle was boiling on the stove, so I went over to it and hit this maid around the head. I was screaming at her how he was mine, not hers. The scalding water was all over her. Screaming in agony, she was. Then I ran. Ran as fast as I could into the wood." Esme is back in that moment even now, wanting this maid dead.

"How long were you in the woods, Esme?" I wanted to know her innermost feelings from that night.

Esme is now explaining in a whisper, "I stayed there all night and all the next day, crying and thumping the mossy ground beneath me. I could see no way out. I wanted to end this misery I was feeling. I planned that night to find peace."

I now knew the next part of her fate, how Leonora had saved her life and nursed her back to physical health. Mentally Esme would never be the same.

"Will it hurt, miss? Will the birthing of this baby hurt?" She is looking scared now as if some sort of reality is starting to set in. I am honest and tell her that it will hurt, and she will be frightened, but all will be well. She will not die. I go on to explain that the doctors and nurses will help her during her confinement. I am praying to God that this will be true. "When will it happen, miss? Please tell me when." I have no answers for dear Esme, only saying it will be at least three months away yet. Esme seems content with my answer and turns her head to one side, drifting off again into a fretful slumber.

Tess is entering the ward now, heading towards the bed. "I have come to take over from you, May. Doctor Fallon wishes to talk with you now. This is your chance to tell him, May."

"Three, two, one. Open your eyes, May, you are back in the present day."

My eyes slowly opened, adjusting to the warm and cosy room. The fire embers were glowing orange, the gold letter opener being put away for the next time.

Chapter 20

1996

The new year 1996 had arrived. The Christmas break a distant memory. It was early in January and it was cold, damp, and miserable. Everyone was fed up with the first morning back at work. Post-Christmas blues having well and truly kicked in, even Maggie and Sandra could not make me smile this morning as they were as fed up as me. Colin looked to be in the depths of depression and any sign of the grinning Colin singing 'Agadoo' by Black Lace had well and truly disappeared. This memory did bring a smile to my face, though.

Nancy was looking as forlorn and upset as she did on the night of the Christmas party. Both Maggie and Sandra awee putting her mood down to being back at work, and I for one was certainly not letting them think any differently. The day plodded on and by lunch time it felt like we had never been away. All service resumed as usual, what with Maggie and Sandra's jokes and sarcasm all back and in fine form by midday. Nancy, on the other hand, was still very quiet. Colin had almost managed to lift his chin off the floor. And me? I was just wishing the week away until Thursday came around and I could find out more about what happened to Esme.

It was now after lunch and Maggie and Sandra came back in from outside, the smell of cigarette smoke following them and clinging to their hair and clothes. "I know just the thing that will cheer us all up and banish them Christmas blues," Maggie gushed, full of excitement. The three of us looked at her to continue. "A night out somewhere. The civic centre puts on a weekly bingo which looks good, and they pay out well too. What do you reckon?"

Of course, Sandra was nodding her approval like one of those nodding dogs in the back of a car window, saying, "Great idea, Maggie."

All eyes were now on Colin and me. "To be honest money is a bit tight at the moment, what with Christmas and everything," Colin replied more confidently than he felt, I am sure.

I chirped in, "Yes, sounds like a fabulous night out. Why don't we leave it until next month when our bank balances have recovered?" I thought this would give me ample time to think of some reason not to go. I was only just getting over the Christmas party, and whilst it was nice to go out occasionally, I did not want to be tied in every month. I had done all my gallivanting in my twenties and was content being a home bird. Give me a good film, bottle of wine, and a takeaway, and I was more than happy on the couch with Steve and the kiddos. Some might say boring, but I say whatever makes you happy. A few times a year was enough for me, and these nights out did not come cheap. "You two could always go to the bingo and suss it out, tell us what it's like," I offered as if I had to justify my reasoning, not wanting to put a damper on things now the mood had lifted. They both seemed happy with this conclusion, as did Colin and I, giving each other a sly look and a smile.

The very next week Colin came in positively glowing, even whistling, which I had never heard him do. "You look like the cat that's got the cream," I said, nudging him in jest.

"I certainly am pleased with myself, or at least I shall be in one month's time," he replied, giving me a grin and a wink.

"Tell me then," I implored, exasperated.

"I have just handed in my month's notice. I've been accepted on the paramedic course at the training base." My heart leapt for him as I knew how much this meant to him.

The pure selfish part of me, however, wished he were not going as I had grown fond of Colin and felt we had built up a good understanding of each other and knew how to handle Maggie and Sandra at last. I wished him well and gave him a hug. What would I do without my friend? As if reading my mind, Colin said, "We will keep in touch always, May. I shall never forget how you took me under your protective wing to guard me from the two pecking hens." We both laughed and embraced again. Colin would make a fantastic paramedic and once the news had sunk in, I really was thrilled for him.

Maggie and Sandra, on the other hand, were not best pleased to hear of Colin's impending departure. Grumbles of "For gawd's sake. Now who we gunna 'ave?" was Maggie's response, closely followed by Sandra adding, "You will have to pick up your pace now, May."

In my defence, I said, "I try my best to be quick, but you two have been doing this for years." They didn't hear me though, as Maggie was too engrossed in who we would be getting next on the production line.

"I bet you any money you like it will be some spotty cocky kid straight ought of school. You mark my words."

Sandra, in parrot fashion as always, added, "Yeah, think she knows it all and will be telling us what to do before we know it."

"Not on my watch, she won't," Maggie spat with venom.

"Let's just wait and see." I tried in vain to reason with them, thinking of some poor unsuspecting young girl or woman being served their fate before they had even had the interview.

Maggie then became quiet and thoughtful, like she had one of her ideas brewing. "Tell you what though," Maggie said.

We all looked at her and replied, "What?"

"This, ladies, will call for a leaving do!"

Colin at once expressed his "I don't want any fuss" spiel. Which of course was not heard as planning was already underway.

"Hey, Nancy. We are having a whip round for Colin's leaving present. A night out is also in order."

Nancy just nodded in our direction, batting her hand at us. "Yes. Yes, OK." Nancy was too preoccupied going through some important-looking paperwork to be interested in what Maggie was saying.

I did manage to have a discreet word with Nancy to ask her how her mother was settling in at the nursing home. Nancy was starting to tell me that her mother had been allowed to go in for one visit over the break, but of course Maggie and Sandra were trying their best to earwig, so I decided to leave things until another more private time.

The weeks soon passed, and it was time for Colin's leaving do. In the end it was Colin's choice for it to just be the four of us. We all had a nice evening at the local Chinese restaurant in town. It was one of those all-you-can-eat places, and I knew before we went that Maggie would be making full use of the offer. She did not disappoint. Somewhere in between overstuffing on the Peking crispy duck and starting on the sweet and sour chicken balls, we decided to give Colin his leaving card and present. Again we kept the collection to the three of us. Mr Gaskill and Nancy also put some money in the pot for the gift. I oversaw making sure that Mr Gaskill and Nancy signed the card and thought it would be a nice gesture if I got all the other factory girls to write in the card as well. This did not go down well when Maggie and Sandra noticed all the good luck and farewell messages that filled the card. They both agreed I should not have let them write in it as they didn't contribute to the buying of it. Honestly, I could not do right for doing wrong with these two at times. "Give me strength," I said under my breath.

Colin enjoyed his meal out and the present that we had bought him: a fishing voucher from the local tackle shop so he could put it towards a new rod and reel that we had overheard him saying he needed. We promised to keep in touch with each other, either meeting up for a coffee or via the telephone. I hugged Colin goodbye, saying through tears, "Don't be a stranger, my friend."

What with Colin leaving our little group, it got me thinking. I too was fed up with the boring routine of this job and I was certainly sick of the sight of biscuits. I had been contemplating for some time finding something new to do. And I felt I knew what that thing was. Ever since going back to the Victorian asylum, I had felt whilst I was there, I had enjoyed immensely trying to help those lost souls. I did not, however, enjoy the treatment received at the hands of the other attendants, and even some of the nurses were cruel. I felt that I could train as a care assistant at the local nursing home, St Joseph's, and hone my skills to be kind and helpful to the patients.

Later that evening, once dinner was out of the way, I spoke with Steve about what was on my mind. Steve being Steve, he was as supportive as ever and said that he would be fine with whatever I decided. I would need to think carefully about this, as I did not want to jump out of the fat into the fire. As if reading my thoughts, the house phone trilled. It was Colin letting me know that a job had become available on the day shift at St Joseph's. Colin had been dropping off a patient there when one of the carers asked him if he knew of anyone to fill the position. He went on to tell me that no experience was necessary as full training would be provided on the job. I could vaguely recall telling Colin some months back that I might like to be a career, but I never in a million years thought that he would remember.

Decision made, I rang the nursing home to enquire about the job and to see if it was still available. The receptionist made some enquiries for me and was pleased to let me know that the position was indeed still available. An interview was arranged for the following morning at 10am. I would need to pull a sickie from the factory or have an impromptu dental appointment. Maggie and Sandra would be having kittens at this rate. I could visualise Nancy and Mr Gaskill having to step in, and I smiled at the thought.

I got up extra early the next morning, dressing in a smart pair of black bootcut trousers and a deep red jumper. I was feeling incredibly nervous, not only at the thought of the interview but also ringing work to say that I wouldn't be in. I hated fibbing and always felt that my voice would give the game away. I decided to go down the toothache route and say I had to see a dentist. That way I thought if I was seen, then that would cover me. And believe me, if I didn't want to be seen this morning, I would undoubtedly be seen by every single person I knew. Sod's law.

"Phew. Thank God that is over with." I was still shaking as I put the receiver down after speaking with Nancy about my dreadful toothache. It was only a semi-lie, I thought to myself, still trying to justify it. I had a dreadfully sore wisdom tooth that needed attention. This was a few years ago, but Nancy didn't need to know that. Dropping Toby and Millie off at school, I kissed the top of both their heads, wishing them both a good day. I wrapped my chunky cardigan around me as even though it was late March, there was still a chill in the air. The further I walked, the more nervous I was feeling. At least if I did not feel it was for me, or they did not feel I was the right fit for them, I hadn't lost anything – well, apart from a day's pay, that is. Nothing ventured. Nothing gained.

Arriving at the nursing home, I was far too early, so I decided to have a walk around the garden. It was small and took me about two minutes to complete. I dared not walk the garden a second time just in case someone thought I was up to no good and called the police, which would not be the best of starts. I headed towards the double-fronted doors that led into the nursing home. Two terracotta pots were either side of the door with a topiary tree planted in each. A light above the entrance was made to look like an old-fashioned lantern, and just above the lantern was a modern-looking security light that suddenly came on and nearly blinded me. It was a dark, overcast day, so the settings had not been adjusted. I had to press a bell that was fixed to the side of the door and then I waited until somebody came to let me in. The waiting did not help my nerves.

Before long, a smartly dressed middle-aged lady came to unlock the door and let me in, but not before asking for my full name and my reason for being there. I thought this a sensible thing to do as there were so many unsavoury characters about. You could never be too careful. I was led in by this lady, who had introduced herself, explaining that she was the receptionist-cum-secretary and "jack of all trades". She told me all this with a warm, welcoming smile, which put me at ease and made me feel less anxious. I was asked to take a seat while this lady went to fetch the matron of the home, who would be doing the interview.

The matron walked briskly down the corridor to greet me, holding out her small soft hand to shake my own. She wished me a good morning and asked me to follow her into her office. The matron was tall with brown bobbed hair, dressed in a navy-blue dress with a matching belt with a gold buckle. Her flat black patent shoes shone brightly against her thick denier tights. The matron did not have the white stiff triangular hat on her head, as you see some of the staff in hospitals wear. However, I did notice it laid on her desk.

I was soon put at ease as the matron was explaining all about St Joseph's and what would be expected of me if I was offered the job as a care assistant. My day would start at 7am and end at 3pm. I would be expected to be on duty at least by 6.45am to hear the night staff giving their handover to the day staff. For the first three months, I would be shadowing an experienced care assistant. This would include my training period, learning the correct way to assist the patients. I would need to attend lifting, handling, and fire lectures and would need to know where the muster point was in the home. Later once I was qualified, I would need to know how to take the patients' observations, known as TPR: temperature, pulse, and respiration. I would be shown how to take the patient's blood pressure both sitting and standing. All of this we would be expected to do once a week to go into their care plan, more often if they became ill.

The matron must have seen the look of bewilderment on my face as she smiled kindly and said, "Please do not look so worried. This would be much further down the line."

Thank God for that, I thought. After the report I would be given a list of patients to help get up, and after sitting them on a commode, I would then be expected to wash them and apply cream to areas that were prone to pressure sores. "The elbows, hips, sacrum, and shoulder blades are the normal culprits along with the back of the heels," the matron explained, adding again for me not to look worried as I would not be expected to take this information in all at once.

"What made you decide that you might like to be a carer?" I was now being asked.

I couldn't exactly say, "Oh, I used to be a carer one hundred and fifty years ago in a lunatic asylum," so instead I opted for the safer option of the usual, "I have always wanted to care for people and help them, and now my children are getting older, I can commit a few days a week."

The interview came to an end and the matron thanked me for coming in, saying what a pleasure it had been to meet me. I parted ways, shaking her hand and saying, "Likewise, Matron."

I would have to wait around a week to see if I had been successful or not as they had another two women they were going to be interviewing, although the receptionist did tell me that she thought that there would more than likely be two vacancies. I was to find out later in my job that many care assistants would either stay for years or stay for days, or even hours.

I was washing up the dishes later that evening when I received a phone call letting me know that I had been successful in my interview and that they would like to offer me the job at St Joseph's. I did not expect to hear back so quickly. My mind was in overdrive. It was now or never. I thanked the manager and accepted the position, explaining that I would have to give one month's notice from my current job.

To say that I was dreading telling the factory girls my news was most definitely an understatement. I arrived the next morning with my notice clutched in my hand. As per usual Maggie and Sandra could be heard before I rounded the corner, only this time there was three of them puffing away on their morning smokes.

"Hiya, May. This is Kate, the newest member to our team of four." I found out that Kate was a dab hand at catching the never-ending stream of custard creams and chocolate bourbons, so much so that Kate took my place, and I assumed Colin's old position. Kate was a middle-aged lady that had always lived locally. I could tell by her accent. She fitted in well, had a great sense of humour, and could swear with the best of them. It made my job easier in telling Maggie and Sandra of my impending departure. They took it well and decided that for my leaving do we were all going to the bingo! Along with Kate. To my utter surprise I enjoyed bingo so much so that the four of us would make it a once-a-month date.

On my last day Maggie and Sandra hugged me tightly, even getting a little emotional. I would miss these two even if they did put the fear of God in me when I first started. I had them to thank after all, because if I hadn't started working at the factory, I never would have met the factory girls, so in turn would never have gone to that hypnotist all those months ago. And, more significantly, would never have had the chance to meet Esme.

Chapter 21

1846

It is a fresh, sunny April morning, and the patients and attendants are gathered in the airing court waiting to go out on our daily stroll around the gardens. We were unable to go the day before due to the constant rain. Beady Eye and Hairy Mole are huffing and puffing, doing their normal grumbling about what a total and utter waste of time this exercise is and how they believe that the patients should be kept in as punishment and how this makes extra work for them.

Gertie is fumbling in the box of hats and shawls, trying to make up her mind on which one to wear. Daphne is a new patient who has no time for Gertie whatsoever and gets extremely cross with her. "Get a move on, will you, daft old bat," she yells scornfully at poor Gertie. This makes Esme wild as she has become increasingly protective of Gertie. Without warning, Esme lashes out at Daphne, whacking her hard around the left side of her head. This burst of sudden fury excites the remaining patients. Some are screaming in what sounds like pain and others are calling out and laughing madly. Two have left our group and are running around the airing courts, scratching at the walls and barking like dogs. Chaos is soon underway and for anyone on the outside of these walls listening in, it really does sound like a mad house. Hairy Mole is sealing her lips around an old tin whistle, the sort that has the dried pea in the opening. The shrill sound of the whistle is enough to bring back some order to the women.

Two of the women are still laughing manically, which does not please Hairy Mole. I am looking at her bright red face, made even redder either by temper or from blowing the tin whistle, or maybe a combination of the two. "Quiet. Shut up," She bellows as she takes in a lungful of air in preparation to blow the tin whistle once more. Her lips seal tighter this time as the hairs on her mole also meet the neck of the whistle. She means business this time. There is a long, loud, sharp blow, so sharp and with such great gusto that I can see a fine mist of spit fly out of her mouth. "Any more of that and you will all be back inside. You are acting more like animals every day."

Now at one time Hairy Mole would not have tolerated this behaviour. She would have had every single one of those patients back inside and no doubt scrubbing floors and cleaning the wards and bathrooms for the rest of the day. Things have been slowly changing in the asylum. I had been called into the expected meeting with Doctor Fallon, and true to his word, he assured me that he wanted to make some improvements. He realises that this will not happen overnight and will more than likely be years in the making. It is a start though. And I for one am in total favour of it.

I found out that Doctor Fallon was to be Doctor Jones' permanent replacement. After thirty years as the chief superintendent, Doctor Jones had decided to retire. During the morning of my meeting with Doctor Fallon, Doctor Jones was also in attendance, looking at his new fresh-faced prodigy. With every new idea and vision that Doctor Fallon had for the patients and staff, Doctor Jones would bite his bottom lip and suck air in through his teeth in equal measures. This wonderful doctor was at last going to change this place for the better. Starting with better treatment of the patients, his belief being that if you showed kindness and care, then in turn the patients would feel less anxious and their hysterical behaviour and unpredictability would occur less often. He added that for the melancholy patients and those that had been brought in with postpartum madness, kindness would help them no end, better than any medicine or cruel conversion therapy ever would.

Doctor Jones did not share this sentiment one bit. "Don't be so darn ridiculous, man. Coming in here, taking over with your fandangle ideas, you are as mad as them." Doctor Jones was of the idea that the only way to cure these imbecilic creatures was to continue with the conversion therapies. "You pay attention. If you get soft with them, they will walk all over you. The lunatics taking over the asylum comes to mind." Doctor Jones really was not best pleased.

The fine new doctor was not backing down, saying quite curtly, "I am the new superintendent, and I shall decide how this establishment is run, and how best I believe to keep order."

I almost felt sorry for Doctor Jones as he looked like a typical little boy had been scolded in public by his mother. He was looking rather flustered by now. His grey hair that was usually slicked back over his head now had curly wispy strands falling forward and skimming his long eyebrows. His face was red like beetroot and his temple veins looked like they could pop at any moment as they throbbed in time with his racing heart. He needed a brandy. His hand was shaking as he took the crystal top off the decanter, trying to pour it now as steadily as he could, the bottle clinking on the glass below. He was losing control of the asylum and in turn all that went along with it. Times needed to change as this treatment was barbaric and evil and cruel. I did not envy Doctor Fallon in his quest to slowly change things as I knew extremely well that two attendants would not be happy.

Now that decorum has been restored, we can continue our walk. I ask Gertie if she is feeling up to the walk, after the upset with Daphne. I really do not think Gertie knows what I am on about and has no memory of the incident, thankfully, as she is in full conversation with Dorothy. "Ah,

147

I really love you, Dorothy. Bless your heart, you do make me laugh," she is saying into the fresh air above her, holding her hands up as if greeting the elusive Dorothy. It must have been a very funny story that Dorothy was telling as by now Gertie's face is soaked with tears of laughter.

We have just gone past the vibrant blue of the hydrangeas that look even more vivid against the lush green grass, when suddenly, we all hear a scream. I look around me and it doesn't take me long to locate where it is coming from. The source of the scream is Esme. Her waters have broken. Even though I have explained many times to Esme about this happening and that it signals the first signs of labour starting, Esme never quite understood things. With Doctor Fallon's blessing, I asked if I could be with Esme throughout her confinement, labour, and birth.

I am taking Esme's hand in mine now, trying to ease her worry. Tess, along with Beady Eye and Hairy Mole, are quickly trying to shepherd the women back into the airing court. Thankfully for most the commotion goes unnoticed, and the ones that do see just think she has wet herself and find this highly amusing, pointing and giggling hysterically at Esme. Esme has no pain at this point, so it could be many hours or even days before the birth. I am leading Esme now by the hand, back towards the dormitory and her bed. I am telling her that she must rest and try to clear her mind of worry as she will need to conserve every drop of energy for the hard work of the labour and birth. *My dear Esme, I hope God is good to you and makes way for an easy passage to bring this new life into this world.* This is something that I keep to myself so as not to tempt fate.

Hairy Mole and Beady Eye both are in the ward now, standing not too far away from the bed. As uncaring and unkind as ever, Hairy Mole says to me, "Good God, girl, stop your fussing. It is a baby being born for goodness' sake; it's not the end of the world. Leave her be. We will have enough to do later with her and her spawn. Making more bloody work for all of us." My God, I hate this woman more so now than I have ever done.

"Will it hurt, miss? I am scared it will hurt," innocent Esme asks me. I always promised Esme I would tell her the truth.

This question she had asked me many times before, and my answer was always the same. "Yes, it will hurt. And labour is exhausting and that is why it is called labour. Your body will know what to do instinctively."

Always one to interfere and butt in, Beady Eye says, "Course it will hurt, you stupid idiot. Imagine the worst pain that you have ever felt and triple it, then that is not even close. Do not be such a baby. Women have been birthing since the beginning of time."

By this time Esme is becoming very unsettled and agitated, bringing her knees up then putting them straight back down, then wriggling about, saying she has a feeling she needs to go to the toilet. Her breathing is laboured, and she keeps on sighing repeatedly like she is hungry for air.

"It is the jitters kicking in, Esme. Please do not worry or take any notice of them two. Neither has ever birthed a baby and have no idea what they are on about."

This eases the situation temporarily. That is until Hairy Mole is ordering me out of the room and saying, "Come on out. You got work to do. Lunch time is getting underway, and we got all the lunatics to toilet yet."

I am feeling brave and dare to say, "I will do no such thing. I am staying with Esme for as long as she needs me. I have been granted permission to do so by Doctor Fallon."

Their response, as expected, is the normal moans and groans of "He has gone too far with his interfering, never had this when Doctor Jones was in charge."

In truth I suspect that they are more fed up as now they have to do things properly, or at least they should. I have my doubts, though, about whether any of the lunch time toileting will be done. Doctor Fallon must be making an impact, as not so many months ago, if I had dared to speak out to either Hairy Mole or Beady Eye like I just had, then I would have been pulled out of the room by the scruff of my collar.

Tess creeps into the dormitory with two pieces of bread and jam, wrapped up in a napkin that she was hiding in her apron pocket. "I will try and bring you a cup of tea as well, May. I will have to bide my time when I am certain that I am not being watched." Tess is so kind and thoughtful.

"Yes, for goodness' sake, don't get caught," I tell her. I just know that both of those awful attendants would love to get Tess into trouble. You can feel their eyes burning holes into you when they are in one of their extra spiteful moods.

I devour the jam and bread quickly, partly because I am so hungry and partly through fear of being caught. I offer Esme a sip of water, helping to lift her head off the pillow. Esme takes just enough water to moisten her parched lips. I ask her if she would care for some soup, to which Esme declines, saying that she is feeling quite sick. "You must try and eat a little, Esme. You need to keep your strength up." Esme shakes her head. I notice that her teeth are chattering more so now. It is not through cold as she feels warm to my touch. No, this is through fear alone. Fear of the unexpected.

The afternoon drags on and there is still no sign of any contractions starting. Esme is in and out of a fretful sleep, stirring now and then. I am sure she is so tired due to all the worry that is consuming her mind. Around 4pm Esme asks for me to help her to the toilet. She is so frightened to be left alone even for a second. Esme has a terrible problem passing anything and explains she is desperately trying to open her bowels, but nothing is happening. Esme has lower back pain now and a slight stomach pain. I am recording this in her notes as I suspect that Esme is in the early stages of labour. Esme shuffles back to bed, still feeling the need to open her bowels. I am now explaining this is the start of labour and not constipation.

The pain is getting stronger now, more frequent. I hear the chapel clock strike six times. Before long the women are being brought into the dormitory to get ready for bed. One of the women is protesting and refusing to go, so Hairy Mole gets hold of her wrist and twists it hard. She is roughly dragging the poor soul by her ear. The woman loses her balance and trips, crying out in agony as Hairy Mole is still dragging her kicking and screaming over to her bed. The extra work has made the two attendants dreadfully bad-tempered. The other women, seeing the rage of Hairy Mole, get into bed as quiet as mice. There is silence in the room, the only noise the faint ticking of the clock. The smell hits me after a few minutes. It is the smell of stale urine and dirt. Now I know that the women who could not take themselves to the toilet have just been left to wet themselves.

Esme is starting to disturb the other women; her labour pains are now in full force. It is time to take her to a side room just off the main corridor. As I lift the sheets off Esme and help her to stand, I notice a watery blood stain on the bottom sheet. "Not to worry, Esme, all perfectly normal." I do not want to alarm her any more than necessary. I have no idea if this is normal or not as I am out of my depth. I am feeling scared myself and I need a midwife.

We pad down the corridor in the dusk of the April evening, the barred windows just allowing enough light for us to see our way. Esme stops every few steps, grabbing at her stomach and leaning against the cold stone wall for support. "Not long now, Esme. Come just a bit further along and we will be there," I encourage her as I know extremely well that if Esme were to slide down the wall and onto the floor, there would be no way that I could lift her up.

As we are entering the room, I recoil slightly. It is filthy, absolutely disgusting. It smells old and damp, and the stone floor has a layer of damp just starting to form on it from the temperature change. Not a bowl or towels in sight. What am I going to do? And more concerning is what is Esme going to do? Just at the back of the small poky room, I notice a door leading, I presume, to another room. I decide that once I have positioned Esme on the bed safely, I shall investigate. There is only an oil cloth for Esme to lay on, no sheets to cover her and only a rolled-up scratchy blanket that I use as a pillow for her head. This room was supposed to be cleaned and ready for a labouring mother and the impending arrival. I can guess who the two lazy culprits are.

Just as I am making Esme as comfortable as I can, the door at the back of the room bursts open with such force that it slams into the wall on our side of the room. A very tall lady comes in briskly and stands at the foot of the bed. I feel relief flood over me. Thank goodness the midwife has come to help Esme. This lady is dressed differently to the other attendants and nurses. She is dressed head to toe in a long black dress with a white apron, the ribbons tied tightly at the back, nipping in at her tiny waste. Black shiny lace-up boots contrast with the white of her underskirt, which is showing about one inch below her hemline. Her hair is jet black with just a few strands of grey starting to show. Her hair is pulled so tightly in a bun that it makes her eyes look slanted. The white crisp cap pinned tightly into her hair does not have frills on like ours do. I look into her eyes, hoping but doubting that I will see even a hint of kindness. Her eyes are the darkest brown I have ever seen, almost black. Soulless. She wears little round glasses pressed tight up to her eyes. One eye looks straight at me and the other appears to have a mind of its own, rolling down into her socket one minute then darting to the top corners. I need to know if she is indeed a midwife or not. "Are you a midwife? Did Doctor Fallon send for you?" I ask in hopeful trepidation.

"I am all you got, girl. I am no midwife, but I delivered enough babies in the convent to put me in good stead. Now

I work as a night nurse here instead. I was a nun." I do not know whether to be relieved or mortified at this latest turn of events. I do not have long to ponder on it as Esme lets out the most blood-curdling scream. I stroke her hair, doing all I can think of to comfort her. As the contraction subsides for a moment, I notice a soft flock laid in the corner of the room. I shall bring that over to lay the baby on. I still do not know this nurse's name and I am too scared to ask her. I decide to call her the Crow as that is exactly what she reminds me of.

Now she is stood nearer the bed, I can see her face more clearly and notice that she has a long, crooked roman nose, very beak-like. She keeps disappearing from our room, complaining that she has other patients to cope with along with Esme. She points her bony bent finger in Esme's direction.

The pain is almost continuous by now and Esme is exhausted. Again, I hear the chapel clock strike 5am. This is a long, painful labour, and I am wondering how much longer Esme can endure it. Two tin buckets have been brought in and one is filled with blood and rags. Is this amount of blood normal? I wonder to myself. The Crow walks in and briskly instructs Esme, "Open your legs and let me see." Esme instinctively clamps her legs shut, which makes the Crow angry. She snaps at Esme cruelly, "You were keen enough to open your legs to receive the seed, so now you can open them to spawn this thing. It is God's way of making you repent your sins and pay for your immoral, loose ways. Disgusting idiot lunatic."

Esme is not responding to these nasty spiteful taunts; she is sleepy and totally worn out. "Please can this poor woman have some chloroform or something for the pain?" I ask in despair.

My question amuses the Crow greatly. "Of course she cannot, stupid girl. It will send her to sleep, and she needs to be awake to push this sin out of her." This woman is on par with the other two, totally heartless. The other bucket is now half full of blood-soaked rags, and I am feeling very worried about Esme. She is so pale, almost transparent.

Next another attendant walks into the room accompanied by the Crow. They are shaking Esme awake and lifting her legs above her in two material slings attached to a device that is not unlike the bath lift. They are shouting at Esme, "Wake up. It is time to push." Esme is still in and out of sleep, and I am trying to rouse her. Her eyes open at last, tired, red, swollen eyes, her auburn hair stuck to her head with sweat. The Crow is being particularly nasty, telling Esme she has one hour to deliver this baby, after which time her shift ends and she will be left all alone with only me to help her. They are whipping her nightdress up now to examine Esme. There is blood everywhere being mopped up by more rags, which smears in circles on the oil cloth beneath. The Crow is down Esme's bottom end, looking for any sign of the baby's head crowning. The younger, slightly nicer attendant is being instructed to place her hands at the top of Esme's belly and push down, applying as much pressure as she can in the hope that it will hurry the birth along. This act has next to no effect, so in earnest the attendant proceeds to add more of her body weight on the stomach. She does this until she is almost sat upon Esme.

At last, there is an earnest yell of, "The head is coming. I can see the head. Push, girl. Push." Esme can barely open her eyes again by now, least of all push. The Crow is now sat in a chair, her feet resting on the foot of the bed, and she is using this to aid anchorage to pull on something with all her might. I realise she is using forceps to tug the baby out.

A shrill cry fills the air, and at last the baby is out. Shrivelled and bright red, head misshapen from the delivery, but it is out finally. I fetch the flock and lay it on Esme's bed, ready for her new baby. The Crow is heading out of the room with this tiny mite, so I shout out, "Where are you taking the baby?" Esme has not even had chance to see it yet or know if she has birthed a boy or a girl. "Wait, bring that baby back at once," I shout, sounding braver than I feel. The Crow turns around and brings the naked, now chilly, baby to me. I notice that Esme has birthed a daughter. Gently I try and wake Esme, and her eyes open slowly. "You have a beautiful daughter, Esme." A small, weak smile appears on her face, her eyes trying to focus on this tiny little girl. I rest the baby on Esme's chest and place her arms around the child, covering them both with the soft flock. "What shall you name her, Esme?" I ask softly.

"Lily. I shall call her Lily."

Esme is so tired her eyes slowly close again, and her arms flop to her sides. I find another blanket in the cupboard and cover Esme over with it. As I do so I notice more blood is slowly oozing out beneath her and dripping onto the floor. "Esme. Esme. Wake up. Are you awake?" Something is desperately wrong with Esme. As I look at her again, she is deathly grey, her lips taking on a hint of blueish-purple. I am screaming loudly for help repeatedly until eventually another nurse whom I do not recognise comes rushing in.

The nurse is now up on the bed on top of Esme, pushing down hard on the top of her stomach. "Has it stopped? Has the blood stopped coming?" the nurse is asking me, looking over her shoulder at me.

I gingerly lift the blanket up with one hand, as I am still holding Lily with the other. "Yes, nurse, it has stopped. Will she be all right?" I hardly dare ask, fearing the reply.

"She has lost a lot of blood. Only time and prayers will help her now."

Shortly after a doctor arrives and gives Esme an examination along with an injection of some sort. He then puts some liquid which I believe is chloroform on a small rag and places it under Esme's nose. He looks across at me, still holding Lily, and tells me, "This woman needs stitching up. She has suffered a third-degree tear which has nearly split her through." My poor Esme. Please, God, I pray to you to save her and protect this little mite.

It is touch and go, the doctor is telling me, and if she survives the day and night, then she will have a chance, as long as she does not develop an infection. That will be nigh on impossible to avoid in this filthy, dirty, rat-ridden place.

After several hours Esme's eyes flicker open, and I smile down at her. "Lily, where is Lily?" Esme asks, concerned.

"She is safe with the nurses just through that door," I say, stroking her head and helping her sip the water that has been left on the side.

"I need to see her. I need to see her one last time." I am alarmed listening to what Esme is saying. Is this baby condemned to the workhouse or an orphanage? Will Esme be allowed to go? Can they stay together? So many questions are running through my mind.

I enter the room behind the birthing room and to my surprise I am met with six children ranging in age from around two to sixteen. Some are rocking on the floor with a foot chain attached, shackled to the wall. The two-year-old is stood up in his cot, looking filthy and malnourished. The rest of the children are sat on the dirty floor playing with pieces of rags, not a toy in sight. I am soon informed by the head nurse that these children have either been birthed by a lunatic or been birthed an idiot and their parents have abandoned them here. I now venture to ask, "What will happen to them?"

The reply from the head nurse is both heartbreaking and callous. "If they do not thrive, the youngest will die. And if God spares them, they will either go to the workhouse or move to the adult wings here. Whatever happens they will never leave and will live out their lives in an institution." They add curtly, "Tis God's will." I ask for baby Lily as her mother would like to see her.

I am now taking this tiny bundle into Esme's room. Still too weak to sit up, I lay Lily on Esme's chest. Esme is smiling now, gently stroking the fine blonde baby hair. She tenderly whispers, "Goodbye, Lily. Goodbye, my sweet child." Planting a single kiss on the sleeping baby's head, a tear escapes her eye. Next Esme is stretching her hand out, searching for my own. She passes Lily back to me and whispers, "Whether I live or whether I die, I want you to take Lily, take her to Leonora in the woods." Esme is still very weak; her lips have lost that blue tinge but are very pale.

"Esme, you will get better, and I shall help you to get out of this place along with Lily."

A single tear runs down her face again as she says, "Goodbye, sweet Lily. Goodbye, my Lily of the valley." Her eyes close again and her head falls back down heavily on the pillow.

I am crying, "Please don't die, Esme, you can't die."

"Three, two, one, come back, May. Come back into the room. You are safe and you are well, back in the present day of 1996."

I opened my eyes slowly, still wiping the tears from my wet face.

Chapter 22

1996

As the first light appeared, I was up already. I had not slept a wink. Today was the first day in my new job at St Joseph's nursing home and I was nervous to say the least. I was to be on duty at 6.45am to hear the handover from the night staff. My hours were 7am until 3pm. I would still be able to collect Millie and Toby from school. In the new year Steve decided to go self-employed and thankfully had plenty of work on, either house extensions or kitchen and bathroom fitting. Steve could do the drop-offs to school in the morning as most people didn't want builders in their house much before nine.

I put on my new uniform which was white with a bright yellow belt that had a silver clasp. Steve had thoughtfully bought me a fob watch, which I pinned to the left-hand side of my uniform, just below the pocket which would hold my pen so I could make notes about how the patients were doing throughout the day. It all sounded very daunting, and I was beginning to wonder if I had done the right thing. *What if I have a Hairy Mole or a Beady Eye as my work colleagues?* I gave myself a talking to for being so silly. But that would just be my luck!

I was placed with a lovely young care assistant called Ember, whom I would be shadowing for a few weeks until the staff thought that I was trained to an adequate standard. Whoever was first on duty in the mornings made up a tray of tea and coffee and took it into the report room. Usually there were ten staff on duty during the day shift, consisting of two senior carers and eight care assistants.

The smell in the small kitchenette was wonderful. All sorts of aromas hit me, toast, porridge, boiled eggs, and even bacon for those patients that had requested it from the main kitchen. Not that I was feeling the slightest bit hungry. I was far too nervous to even think about food. I had packed some sandwiches early that morning, but I highly doubted I would eat them.

Once we had all gathered in the report room, the day senior introduced me to everyone else. I had a lovely warm welcome. "Welcome aboard, May" and "Glad to have you with us." They all seemed a friendly bunch. Once the handover was completed, we were each given a list by the senior of our jobs for that day. We had about seven patients to wash and dress and one bath each to do. Pinned to the notice board in the report room was another list which we were to all look at. It detailed what breaks we were on and what time we were to go. The first coffee break would be at 10am for fifteen minutes followed by another fifteen minutes after the first group of five had returned. It was explained that the breaks were always split into two lots so there was always staff on the floor to look after the patients. Next on the list were the times in which we had our half-an-hour dinner break. Alongside this list there was yet another list of who would be on the assisted feeding table, which was normally two carers. These patients needed to be fed by us and the food was very often liquidised, as many found it difficult to swallow solid food. We were also expected to empty the patients' bins and clean and bleach the commodes, bedpans, and urinal. This was after we had cleaned the wheelchairs.

They certainly run a tight ship, I thought to myself. I just hoped that I could cope, let alone remember what I was supposed to be doing. As if reading my mind, Ember said kindly, "Don't worry, it isn't half as daunting as it all sounds. You will soon be doing it with your eyes closed." I

159

wanted to say, *yes, my eyes closed with tiredness, no doubt.* Instead, I smiled.

The first patient on our list was an elderly lady called Dora. I liked the way Ember woke this lady up as she very gently touched her shoulder whilst saying, "Good morning, Dora. Are you ready to get up?" Dora nodded, saying that she was. The curtains were pulled open and then Ember walked over to the wardrobe, sorting out a skirt and a blouse, all the time asking Dora which she would like to wear.

Ember explained that the patients were to always be given a choice, whether that be on what to wear or what they would like to eat. I saw how Ember had filled the basin with lovely warm water and added a squirt of bubble bath to it as well.

Next I watched how Ember gently pulled the sheet and blankets off Dora and pointed out how Dora wore an incontinence nappy. I concentrated on what Ember was showing me. The front of the nappy was undone and pushed gently flat on the bed; next we very carefully sat Dora up on the edge of the bed. Ember pointed out to me that this patient had arthritis so was very sore and stiff, especially first thing in the morning. "We give Dora a minute or two just to get her bearings. We do this with all our patients. Nothing worse than being pulled out of bed and onto the commode when you are still half asleep." I agreed with this wholeheartedly and thought what a kind young lady Ember was. She could only be in her early twenties, long brown hair tied back in a ponytail. She was very tall and slim with the most relaxing soft voice that I had ever heard, very well spoken with the loveliest manner and kindest smile.

As we helped Dora onto the commode and made sure that she was comfortable, Ember then put a large soft fluffy towel over Dora's bare legs. "This is to cover Doras's dignity and to keep her as warm as possible. We do this with all our patients. I will show you as we go on." I was listening carefully, not wanting to miss a thing. A flannel was passed to Dora, who liked to wash her own face on the days she felt able to. Once her nightie had been removed, another towel was wrapped around the patient's top half. Dora had a lovely wash and once her teeth were cleaned and hair brushed, we went to our small kitchenette to write the name of the patient that was ready on a list so the unit assistant knew that Dora was ready.

Next it was back into Dora's bedroom where I was shown how to make a bed properly along with hospital corners. Beds had to be stripped and remade. Full change was once per week unless soiled, in which case it would be done at once. The final steps in finishing Dora's morning routine were taking the juice jug, washing it out, and replenishing its contents. Medication was to be administered next, which would have been left in the galley pot by the senior carer. Ember explained the importance of fluids and how they must be encouraged every time we did our checks. "It helps to reduce the chances of developing a UTI." I must have looked blankly at Ember as she smiled as she said, "Sorry, May, a UTI is also known as a urinary tract infection. You will soon pick up the lingo, don't worry."

Each patient took around half an hour to wash and dress. How was I ever going to be able to do all that in half an hour? God only knew. The bathing of a patient took even longer.

Finally, 10am came and Ember and I were on the first coffee break, and I must admit I was feeling a tad peckish by now. Amazingly we had finished our list just in time for 10am. The other four carers were already in the kitchen pouring boiling water out of a big iron boiler which they called an urn. We all mucked in and made the drinks as quickly as we could as if we dilly-dallied, it would eat into our break. Toast was popping from the four-slice toaster and another lot quickly put in. I had never smelt toast like it.

Wonderful. Now whether this was because I was so hungry or not, I do not know, but even now when I smell toast, I am brought back to that kitchen at St Joseph's. Ember explained that if I wanted some toast, I was to make sure that I wrapped it up in a serviette, put it in my pocket, and ate it discreetly as the main boss didn't like us eating his food.

"What, not even a slice of bread?"

Ember's reply was a simple "Nope." I understand all these years later as it would have cost a small fortune to feed all the staff as well, but at the time I moaned and grumbled with the rest of them.

Next on our agenda after morning break was the emptying of the wastepaper bins in the patients' bedrooms, then putting the laundry away. This had to be folded neatly and not just thrown in the drawers, as the matron would continually remind us daily. In between doing all our chores, we still had to answer any call bells that went off, letting us know that someone needed our help.

Lunch was served at 12.30pm, so at around midday us carers had to start the toileting of the patients that could not do it themselves. Starting in the dayroom, Ember and I gathered the wheelchairs ready and one by one we would wheel the patient to the toilet, deposit them on the toilet, then go back into the dayroom to gather the next one in another wheelchair and put them outside the occupied toilet to wait as we went in to rescue the patient off the loo, changing their nappy if needed. And so this would go on until they were all toileted and seated in the dining room. It really was like a relay race and by the end of my time at St Joseph's, I could have named most of the patients by their bottoms!

I was worn out and it was only just dinner time. How was I going to keep this up? After the patients had eaten, the whole procedure of toileting would start again. On the toilet. Off the toilet. Repeat. The ones that wanted to stay in the dayroom were quite content to have a catnap or watch the television. Weather permitting, some would like to sit outside for a while and some would want a cigarette, which we would have to supervise. Some of the more poorly patients who had swollen legs, pressure sores, or such like had to have one hour's bedrest on the orders of the district nurse who would visit once a week. By the time we had put the last one into bed, it would be time to get the first one back up.

When our lunch break came around, I for one was grateful. My legs were killing me, and my feet were throbbing. I could feel them pulsating they were so hot. There was no let up in the afternoons as the next day's menu had to be filled in and the drinks trolley had to be taken around all the patients and visitors. Helping to drink their cups of tea or coffee was a slow job and one that could not be rushed as the patients would cough and splutter if it went down the wrong way.

Finally at around 2.45pm we had time to sit with the patients and chat, either with those in their bedroom or those in the dayroom. It didn't really matter if we chatted. This was one of my favourite parts of the job and not just because it gave me five minutes off my feet. I really enjoyed listening to all the interesting tales that I got told over the years, the lives that they had lived, and funny stories that they remembered. Many of our patients had dementia and would get very confused, wondering where they were and when they would be going home. We would explain repeatedly that they lived here with us now and would not be going home just yet. They all seemed to be accepting of this explanation until five minutes later when they would ask the same question again.

At last 3pm came around and we all gathered by the clocking-in machine to bid farewell to each other with shouts of "See you tomorrow." Ember touched my arm, asking me how I thought my first day had gone.

"I really enjoyed it. I am tired though." I wasn't fibbing and although tired didn't come close to how I was feeling, I really did enjoy my first day. I thought to myself on my way to pick up the children that it wasn't so much the physical work that had tired me but the mental toll of trying to remember everything that I had been told. I was especially worried in case I forgot to write something down in my notes or forgot to fill in the fluid charts. This wasn't a few broken biscuits that I was dealing with but real people.

Later that evening as I flopped down on the sofa, I felt content and happy and had a good feeling about St Joseph's. "Wake up, love, your favourite programme is about to start," Steve said as he was prodding me awake.

In bed I was thinking how different things were now compared to what I had seen in the Victorian asylum. Kind and caring staff always putting the patients first, helping them to eat their meals, helping them to the toilet, and making sure that they were kept dry and changed regularly. Such a vast difference. I would like to think that maybe Doctor Fallon had played a small part in the start of better things to come in the treatment of patients living in care homes, as years ago all these patients would have probably ended up in that institution or somewhere similar, especially if they had no family to take care of them. I slept well that night, only being interrupted by dreams about Esme and her newborn baby. I needed desperately to help this young woman. More so than ever after today.

I had been at the home for eight weeks when the matron called me into her office. I was so relieved and pleased when she told me I had passed my probation period and that she had heard excellent things about me from both staff and patients alike. So pleased she was with me that she didn't need me to do the usual three-month probation period. The cynical part of me believed I only had two months as they were always short-staffed and could ill afford me shadowing Ember and the other carers any longer than I needed to. I had taken to the job well and Ember was correct in her inkling that it wasn't as daunting as I first thought. I still had a lot to learn, like taking the patients' TPR weekly and filling in care plans, but for now they were happy I was there helping. There was plenty of time to learn all the other jobs. I had mastered catheter care along with the fitting of convenes and incontinence care, for which I received a certificate. I was over the moon, and anyone would have thought that I had won a gold medal in the Olympics. I did not care one bit what anyone thought, though, as I had never received a certificate in anything in my entire life.

Chapter 23

1846

The day is dawning, overcast with drizzling rain. I can smell it has rained before I look out of the barred windows. My window opens just enough to let a bit of air in, but not enough to escape through. I dress quickly and head straight down to where I had last seen Esme not many hours before.

Esme is at last sleeping soundly, and the bleeding has stopped, so I make the decision to leave her to rest whilst I get a couple of hours sleep. Not that I manage much sleep due to the traumatic events of the previous twenty-four hours. I open the door as slowly and as quietly as I can. Esme is not in the bed, not anywhere in this cold, sparse room. Panic sets in instantly, starting in the pit of my stomach then creeping up to my throat. It feels like the top of my head is on fire, the panic trying to escape me in one huge explosion. "Esme. Esme. Where are you?" I cry to myself repeatedly. I know she won't answer; it is more for my benefit. I just know she has gone and need to find out where she has been put.

I go into the back room, known as the nursery, I now realise. The scene is much the same as before and I doubt very much if any of these children have been put to bed as each child is in the exact same position. The toddler in the cot is still standing up with outstretched arms as if in search for something or someone. I can't tell if the child is a boy or a girl as the hair is long and matted. A comforter is in its mouth, which has sores either side, reaching up to scabby flushed cheeks. The child's raggy nappy is hanging off, soaked through with urine and dirt. I feel sick, the desperation building within me with every look at these poor innocent mites.

The two that are around six are still shackled. I approach and kneel beside them, asking them now where the nurses are. They stare at me blankly, no idea what I have said. A wild look comes into their eyes. All of a sudden, a slow and steady growl starts within them, getting louder and louder to a pitch that makes me step away from them and cover my ears. They are now trying to stand, but the chain is so tight to the wall they can't manage it. Bent over like prehistoric men, they continue to growl and shout at me. They are feral and not used to human interaction. I notice on the far side of the room there is a table with cups of water and a half-cut loaf of bread. I take the decision to bring the water and bread over to these young boys. I slowly walk over to them and as carefully and as unthreateningly as I can, I place them in front of them. Instantly they both start to rear up at me again, a deep growl coming from their throats, spit spilling from their mouths. I am wondering if it is the sight of a morsal of food that is making them dribble. They do their best to try and reach the bread and water, but it is still just out of reach. I am nudging it over closer to them now. They sniff the bread and the water. They repeat this three times. To my horror they then start to lap at the water, their tongues long and sharp as they poke them out as far as they can to reach inside the cup. The bread they devour like hungry wild dogs, eating it bent over as if they have never used their hands. I can feel my heart thumping against my ribs, the blood rushing to my head. Never have I witnessed such a sight. The animals at home were treated like kings compared to this. Sickening, evil place. I can smell the evil emitting from the dark, damp, repressive walls, the tears running in torrents down the peeling paint. Once finished, the two boys sit back against the wall as if exhausted from the sheer effort of eating.

The door opens now, and a nurse and young attendant are walking in towards me. "What do you think you are doing, girl?" the nurse snaps briskly at me.

"I am here to see Esme and baby Lily. I would like to see them both now, please."

This confidence in my voice isn't going down well with the nurse as she barks back at me, "Well, you can't. Esme is not here, and the baby is to stay in our care."

I look again around this dirty room. "Then can you tell me where Esme has gone?"

The nurse's reply is just a glare and nothing more.

The toddler is still standing struck dumb in its cot. I realise the poor thing has given up crying as nobody ever comes. I look again at the two boys, who by this time have their eyes closed. As if reading my mind, the cruel nurse says, "No good looking at them like that. They are to be held here until the age of sixteen, then they will be taken to the padded rooms to begin their cure."

I cannot help but express my disgust. "That's another ten years away at least. They cannot be expected to live like this for ten years."

The reply I receive is as shocking as the sight of the wild boys. "They are not six, you stupid idiot girl. They are both fifteen. We'll only be holding them another year if that."

These young children are so wild and underfed they only look six. To think they are almost grown men makes my stomach lurch one more. "I would like to see Lily now, and if I don't, I shall have no option but to report you to both the matron and Doctor Fallon."

The nurse scowls at me but nods at the young attendant, adding, "The illegitimate child is through there on the block."

I gasp. "On the block? What on earth is the meaning of this?" I utter, hardly daring to hear the response.

"It's called the thrive or die block. If they live the first forty-eight hours after birth, they live, and if they show signs of weakness, then they will perish, and it will be God's will."

I feel appalled and disgusted with this evil woman. I fear I may hit her if I stay in this room with her any longer. I look across at the attendant and nod to prompt her to take me to Lily. As we both enter another small room, the young attendant grabs my arm, not in an aggressive manner but more in desperation. "Please help me. Get me out of this awful godforsaken place." The girl's face is ashen with worry and despair. I have enough to deal with just trying to help Lily.

Not wanting to upset this girl any more than necessary, I choose my words carefully. "I will try, but it will take some time," I try to reassure her. I mean it, too. As soon as I can, I am going to make sure that Doctor Fallon knows about this evil room.

I look for Lily in the small, dark, cupboard-like room with no windows. The only glimmer of light is coming from a flickering candle, the wax melting down to nothing. My eyes take time to adjust as I look around the room, desperately searching for a glimpse of Lily, my ears straining for the slightest noise. Something catches the corner of my eye, so I move closer to the corner of the room. What has caught my eye is a little white bare leg, barely moving but for a slight twitch. "Lily," I whisper quietly, scooping this cold naked bundle up into my arms. My arm is wet as I look down. I can see that her rag of a nappy is falling off as it is so soaked through. No wonder this little helpless mite is so cold and pale. I am holding her tightly to me now, and just her little head is free. I need to get her warm and dry. Instinctively Lily is opening her tiny mouth and turning her head towards my breast as if searching for the goodness of a mother's first milk. I take my apron off and wrap Lily up, trying my best to get her warm.

I am back in the nursery now and face to face with the cold, callous nurse. "Where do you think you are going, girl?" she says to me scornfully.

My reply is swift and to the point. "I am taking Lily to be cared for in another part of the asylum. This baby needs a wet nurse before she starves to death. She is not staying here a moment more than she needs to." I have no idea where I am going with this wee mite, only my sheer determination is driving me to get her help. I end up outside the matron's office and give a half-hearted knock on the panelled door. My heart is thumping, the rush of blood I feel going to my head. I do not know if I want the door to open or not. What will become of Lily if no one answers? I do not have long to fret as the door swiftly opens to a rather flustered-looking matron. This is most unusual as normally Matron is every bit the unflappable professional. Matron is ushering me in now, motioning with her hand for me to step forward. I notice paperwork in untidy piles on the table and one of the larger chairs.

"What is it, miss? I have work to do and do not have the time for any more problems. Now be quick and spit it out." My stomach feels as though it will come out of my mouth there and then if I open it to speak. I say nothing. Instead I kneel on the rug in front of the glowing fire and start to unravel this little bundle that I have been keeping warm in my apron. Shock and bewilderment are on Matron's face in equal measures, and for a minute or two, her mouth opens and shuts with no words coming out, a bit like a fish out of water.

Eventually Matron finds her voice. "Where did you find it?" she asks, pointing at the bundle on the rug.

"She is Esme's, and she needs a wet nurse and to be taken somewhere safe until her mother has improved."

By now Matron has wondered off to the other side of the room, pouring herself a large spirit which I imagine is brandy judging by the dark rich colour. "I need to think. Let me think. This is all I need."

Now this is not the matron I have come to know; she seems flustered. Dare I ask her what is wrong? I decide to chance it. "Is everything quite all right, Matron? You do not seem to be fully yourself today."

With that Matron's head turns swiftly in my direction and for a split second I think she is going to hit me, so much so that I cower, holding my hands out in front of me. "No, I am certainly not all right. Not all right at all. And it is no thanks to that new Doctor Fallon." She adds bitterly, "And where is he now? Not here helping me sort this lot out, that is for sure." I am sure I see her wipe a tear away from her face.

"Whatever has happened?" I carefully ask, thinking to myself that I have gone this far – in with a penny and all that. Matron can hardly contain herself, as if saying it out loud has really annoyed her. What has Doctor Fallon done or not done? I wonder. I do not have to wait long for Matron to spill the beans. It conspires that an inspection of the entire asylum is going to be taking place any day now. The trouble with this was that when old Doctor Jones was in charge, he always managed to stall the inspection. The one time an inspector did pay a visit unannounced, Doctor Jones plied him with brandy until this chap was in such a drunken stupor he couldn't stand, let alone walk. The matron and the doctor had made the inspector a makeshift bed up on the chaise longue in the office until he had sobered up, then of course the inspector was terrified that the staff would report him. The crafty doctor had built up a nice plan, telling the inspector he was to give an excellent report on the asylum and that it was all due to the head superintendent Doctor Jones' excellent leadership skills that the asylum was running as efficiently and orderly as it possibly could. It was a done deal of course, and no more would ever be said about it. A "you scratch my back, and I'll scratch yours" scenario. Now of course with the old doctor long gone and with the new Doctor Fallon in place, it was time for another one. Finally.

"Leave the baby with me. I shall take it back to the nursery. Now leave me in peace and get out."

I stand my ground and simply say, "No." I decide I have to play my devious card now. My blackmail ace card. "If you don't take me this minute, then I shall have no choice but to tell the staff about the inspection and believe me when I say that the other attendants won't hold back on the misery this place brings to both the staff and patients." I want to run. Run away as fast as possible.

The matron is scarlet with rage; even the top of her forehead is red. "Very well. Mrs Ridley has not long birthed and is in her confinement in the holding ward. She will feed it. And if you dare to breathe a word about this, I will make your life hell." My life is already hell, but I decide just to nod in agreement with her.

I have heard lots about the holding ward from Tess. It is a ward for women who have temporary insanity for several reasons. Mrs Ridley is one of these women who have gone quite mad during their pregnancy, so mad in fact that her husband could not cope with her at home. It is thought that once she has delivered, her mind will return to being sane.

We head out of Matron's office, only stopping so she can lock her office door. No way is anyone getting in there until she returns. Huffing and puffing down the dimly lit maze of corridors, we arrive at the holding ward. This ward is marginally better than the other wards, calmer and much cleaner. No smell of urine or faeces. The women gather in corners talking or reading quietly; there is a different atmosphere. We soon locate Mrs Ridley and Matron leans over her, whispering something in her ear. Mrs Ridley duly nods, and I am told to hand Lily to her. I do so apprehensively, carefully passing this baby over as if she is my very own. Lily latches on immediately to Mrs Ridley's breast, guzzling hungrily, her little eyes shutting with contentment.

"I must get back. Will you make sure you take it back to the nursery? I cannot stand here all day mollycoddling someone else's illegitimate offspring."

I am nodding now in agreement. "Yes. Yes, of course I will." My first plan of action is complete.

I turn to Mrs Ridley and ask if she can keep Lily for a while as I need to find her mother. "Of course I can. I love babies." Now to put my second plan in motion. But first I need to try and find Esme.

I search and search for hours for her but am coming up against lots of doors blocking my way. Nobody has seen Esme, and my time is running out to rescue Lily. If I do not act soon, it will be too late. Changing my plan, I decide to take Lily then come back to find Esme.

I have a rare afternoon off tomorrow, my one and only in about a month. I need to keep Lily with Mrs Ridley for as long as possible. Then after a feed, I will take her into my bedroom and somehow keep her quiet. Then the hardest part, smuggling her out of this hell hole, and on to find Mrs Loney in the woods.

"Three, two, one. May, time to come back into the room. You are fully aware of where you are, and you are safe and well."

"Why can't I find Esme? Where is she?"

Mark didn't know, of course, but he reassured me we would try to find her next time. My greatest fear was that Esme was gone. That my dear Esme was dead.

Chapter 24

1996

I was now placed on a different ward at St Joseph's. We all had to take turns moving around the nursing home so that we could work in all departments should the need arise, such as sickness or staff holidays. This ward was known as the dementia and mental health ward. On this ward we had fifteen patients, all needing extremely high levels of care. It was a secure locked unit as dementia patients were known to wander. I had two doors to unlock to gain access. Once the first door had been unlocked, we had to lock it behind us, and then we were in what the staff nicknamed "The Airlock", a tiny space with nothing in. Once we had unlocked the second door, you were in the unit. It was all for safety in case a patient was to escape. In the case of an emergency, a main lock could be activated, and all doors would be unlocked automatically.

On my first morning on the unit, I was having my morning cup of tea waiting for the night staff to do the handover. Two older carers were sat opposite me, immaculately dressed in their bright white uniforms. Even the seams had been ironed in a perfectly straight line. They must have been in their late sixties at least.

One of the carers, whose name was Sally, asked me if I was the woman who worked at the factory. "Yes, I am indeed. Why do you ask?" I enquired, intrigued.

They looked at each other and smiled. "We used to work there when it was the old mental health unit." They went on to explain that they were the very last members of staff to stay at the old asylum until it closed for good in the late eighties. "We stayed right to the end, brought some of the patients across here with us." It transpired that the old asylum, which was latterly known as a secure unit for the mentally ill, was to close, as had many over the years. Many of these existing patients were put out into the community, known as care in the community, whilst the remaining patients eventually moved across to St Joseph's when the building was complete. "Yep, that was a sad day for us, wasn't it, Monica?"

Monica agreed. "It certainly was. The end of an era."

I had so many questions for them both, so many that I could not decide which one to ask first. I stayed silent and let them continue reminiscing. "We signed our names on the beams right at the very top of that building. That part is still there as part of the biscuit factory." Sally was looking thoughtful as she explained.

Monica added, "Yep, we left our mark. About five or six of us carers signed them beams on the last day. Tears running down our faces." My stomach somersaulted as I remembered going up in that lift all those months ago and looking at those initials, running my fingers over the rough splintered wood.

I went onto the ward after handover, shadowing Sally so she could introduce me to the patients and give me a rundown of their care needs. Each patient had a care plan that we could refer to and update as and when needed. One patient on our rounds was a chap called Jack. I noticed after spending a few minutes with him that his tongue was rolling about his mouth and poking out intermittently. His legs were never still and seemed to be jerking as if they had a mind of their own. Sally explained that this condition was called tardive dyskinesia and was a result of taking long-term antipsychotic drugs to treat mental health conditions, one being schizophrenia. Jack was a lovely man and was one of the patients who had moved over to St Joseph's when the old secure unit shut.

I met many more patients like Jack who had been treated with drugs that had lasting side effects. Another patient was a kindly lady called Miriam who had the most peculiar walk, a tip-toe scuffing walk, like she could trip over her own feet at any moment. I learned that in the nursing profession this was known as the Largactil shuffle, another antipsychotic drug used to treat various mental health problems.

Another two patients I came across in the unit were well into their nineties. I noticed they had dents in either side of their heads. I remember feeling chilled to the bone when Sally went on to explain that these two patients had been residing at the old unit for many years and that the dents were a result of a procedure called a lobotomy where a surgeon would drill a hole in each side of the skull to cut through brain tissue. The other procedure was called a transorbital lobotomy whereupon the surgeon entered through the eye socket. I felt horrified. It was like something out of a horror film to hear of this. Thankfully, these procedures started going out of favour in the fifties. Lasting damage had been done, though, and many were left zombified and a shell of themselves. I found it incredibly hard to know of the horrors that these people had gone through. The others that were released into the community did not fare well either, as most had been institutionalised for most if not all their lives. Not being able to cope with the everyday chores such as cooking and cleaning, they all ended up in care or, in some cases, prison. Care in the community failed and was soon scrapped for mental health patients unless there was a huge care package put in place, which cost money.

Once I had got to know the patients and their quirks, I very much enjoyed working on this unit. One sweet old lady who was ninety-nine years old had the most awful leg ulcers, red raw and what we carers referred to as sloughy. The leg was oozing puss and was infected. The district nurse came and instructed us to use a dressing called Intrasite, which came in a small pouch with a nozzle that you squeezed into the wound. We were then told that the longer the dressing stayed on, the better the healing would be. "How will I know though, nurse?" I asked.

"Trust me, you will know," came the reply from the district nurse, followed by a wink. She wasn't wrong as about three days later as I peeled back the cover to get Violet up, I was hit by the most revolting smell of rotting onions. Panicking the ulcer had had turned gangrenous, I rushed to get Sally.

"Does it smell of rotten onions?" Sally asked me.

"Yes." That was the perfect description of the awful pungent smell that the leg ulcer was emitting. Now I knew that all was well and not to panic, I had to go about redressing the leg. One thing that worked wonders on leg ulcers was a solution called potassium permanganate that we used to soak and gently wash the ulcers in. It was a deep purple, almost black crystal or powder that we were to dilute in water. Whilst I washed and dressed Violet's leg ulcer, it gave me a good chance to have a natter with her.

I would admire all Violet's trinkets that she had dotted around her room, including a dream catcher hanging in her window, which had a tiny little crystal in the middle of it that would cast a prism of all colours of the rainbow. I felt it very calming and could watch it for hours if I had the time. Little crystal stones littered her windowsill, and each one had a different name and had great healing properties within them. According to Violet, each stone could treat or help a different condition. Violet would tell me how much she loved nature and would walk in the woods for hours upon hours. Sitting in the shade under an oak tree or paddling in the shallows of the river. "In nature you will find a cure for just about anything," Violet would often say.

I really enjoyed working on this ward and taking the patients on walks around the small garden. We took our group of fifteen on regular walks, weather and staff permitting, of course. It was on one of these very first walks that I noticed an overgrown patch of wasteland just on the outside perimeter of the nursing home. I asked Sally what it was. It looked like it had just been left and was not part of the home nor the housing development either as it had a small latch gate leading to it from our side in St Joseph's and a wire fence enclosing it. "That is the unmarked graves of some of the old staff and patients from the asylum. Some are well over one hundred and fifty years old, only marked by a number on an old rusty iron peg." It made me incredibly sad to think that all these lost abandoned souls were laying deep under the ground. Forgotten. Sally went on to tell me that when the patients passed away and their families were informed of their death, they often did not claim the body, hence why it was buried in a pauper's grave here. Sally told me to poke my head over the gate and look to my left. There in the overgrowth I could just see a stone building of some sorts. "This was a chapel and part of the old asylum. They couldn't build on this site just in case the relatives of the deceased ever came back to claim them. The numbers on the graves were recorded somewhere and probably held at the library. I couldn't see how many graves were there, but it certainly looked like over one hundred at a quick glance. This was something that I would explore later, and it would throw up a shock or two, that is for sure.

One lunch time after we had toileted the patients that couldn't toilet themselves, we headed into the small comfy dining room. With only fifteen patients it didn't need to be big. There was always such a lovely feel to the room. We would put the radio on, normally BBC Radio 2 as it had both talking and music which we all loved. The soup trolley was then wheeled out and us carers would stand in line with an empty bowl in hand whilst the kitchen assistant ladled out the soup into the bowls. One lunch time all the patients were tucking into their dinner of cottage pie; some had finished before others and on this occasion, Bill was one of the first to finish. Fran, one of the other carers, duly took his plate away and scraped what was left into a big black dustbin which would go for pig's swill. All hell broke loose as Bill started to wave his hands in the air shouting, "Hey, Fran. Me teeth. Me teeth. Me teeth were on that plate." By this time Fran and Bill's teeth were long gone. I hurried into the kitchen, trying to find Fran so I could tell her. I could still hear Bill's shouts of "They cost me a bloody lot of money, them did. That carer better find 'em" in his thick Yorkshire dialect. I shall never forget the sight of Fran, rubber glove and all, scooping through the slop, like she was rummaging through a bran tub searching for a prize – only this prize nobody wanted.

After some time, Fran appeared red-faced from all the bending. "I found them. I found Bill's teeth." We all cheered, but Bill's cheer was the loudest. It was little incidents like this that made the job even more enjoyable. That was unless you were in Fran's position. We all made sure we double-checked the plates from then on.

One of the patients was only in her forties and would smoke continuously if we allowed her to. We would normally let the patients smoke as and when and let the ones who were more carful smoke unsupervised in their rooms. This was before the smoking ban. The ones that were prone to forgetfulness and confusion we would sit with to make sure there were no burns or a fire didn't occur.

This young woman's family did not want her smoking so much, as she would easily get through sixty-plus per day if we let her. So, it was decided by her family that we would allow her forty to start with and then gradually cut it down. We did not get a minute's peace as this lady would constantly ask for a cigarette. She only had to catch a glimpse of a white uniform and at once she would ask, "Can I have a ciggie, please, nurse? Can I?" I went to bed many a night with those words ringing in my head.

Another chap whose name was Ralph had been extremely high up in the army and had suffered the most horrendous shell shock which he never fully recovered from. He was a tall man with thinning white hair and a tiny little moustache, very well spoken. A typical English gentleman. His wife could no longer cope with his mental health problems and, on top of this, he had developed dementia as well. He came onto our unit because he was at considerable risk of wandering off. His wife would come in most days and visit him, bringing us carers a box of chocolates or cream cake each, which was a proper treat. The lady, Mrs Ralph as we called her, suddenly stopped visiting. One morning when Sally came on duty, she had some sad news for us all. "Mrs Ralph has passed away very suddenly. They suspect a massive heart attack." We all took a moment for the news to sink in and to give Mrs Ralph a few minutes in our thoughts.

Whilst we were used to death on a regular basis, we normally had time to prepare the family and ourselves. When it was unexpected like this, it was bound to be a shock all round. The couple didn't have a family and doted on each other. It was down to us to break the news. Ralph was of course beside himself with grief. For about two minutes, that is, then he had forgotten. It was so sad to see Ralph grieving repeatedly like this as he would continually ask, "Where is my wife? Has anyone one seen her today?" To start with we would gently explain that his dear wife had passed away and was no longer with us. Poor Ralph, it was torture for him and like hearing the news for the first time every time we told him. We had a meeting about how best to manage this situation and Matron thought it best if we just told him very casually each time he asked, "Oh yes, Ralph, she is visiting later." We all agreed that this was an effective way forward. I am pleased to say that this harmless lie worked. Whilst Ralph would still continually ask where his wife was, he seemed content with the "She will be in later" answer. It certainly saved Ralph's tears and anguish, and ours too.

One patient we were looking after was called Vera. Vera was a force to be reckoned with and it was a long time before I was allowed to help her. Vera was one hundred years of age, and despite this grand age she still had the strength of an ox. She had a vicious temper and would regularly throw cups of tea or coffee at the carers, a remote control, anything and everything she could get hold of. She always had to be cared for by two carers. She would spit and try and scratch the carers and pull their hair. She really was hard work. The doctors and psychiatrist had tried every drug known to man and nothing dulled her temper. She was not noticeably big, but my God she was mighty.

The time came for me to have a go, with the assistance of Sally. Being the most experienced and senior carer, she would know exactly what to do and how to train me in dealing with this old lady. Vera, as I mentioned, was not very big in stature but quite round and tubby. She had a good head of hair and a full, plump face. I knew this as Sally had given me her patient profile to study so I could get a feel for her needs before I met her. In Vera's notes I noticed that she had one daughter who was next of kin. I did a double take when I saw the daughter's name. Nancy Pickering's name jumped out at me as if she was in the page herself, grabbing hold of me. Could it be the same Nancy from the factory? It had to be as she had told me all about her mother being in a nursing home. Once I had the chance, I asked Sally, who confirmed my thoughts. "Yes, Nancy from the factory. That's correct, May." Sally went on to explain how Vera had treated Nancy appallingly over the years, and that once Nancy could not look after her ailing mother anymore, Vera went crazy at her, hit her and everything. Up until recently Vera refused to see her daughter at all. Nancy never gave up trying though despite all those years of neglect and harsh treatment from her mother. For some reason Nancy stayed loyal. "God knows why," Sally added.

"Time to meet Vera. Are you ready, May?" Sally cajoled.

"As ready as I will ever be, I guess." My stomach was in knots, and I was dreading going into this elderly woman's room.

Sally knocked the door and went in first, saying to Vera, "I would like to introduce you to one of our carers, Vera. Her name is May."

I nervously entered the room and slowly walked around to the front of Vera's chair. "Hello, Vera. Nice to meet you," I said politely, hoping to be in her good books straight away. Vera grunted something at me. As she slowly lifted her head to look at me, I gasped aloud, and my legs turned to jelly immediately. Staring back at me was a cruel, mean, and harsh-looking face. Along with a pinched and thin mouth. Sat just above her lip was a remarkably familiar sight. A huge hairy mole! Could this be Hairy Mole's daughter? I felt faint and as if time had stood still. I would need to talk to Nancy to confirm or deny my suspicions.

Chapter 25

1846

The time has come. Now or never. I manage to keep Lily with Mrs Ridley for the rest of the day. The holding ward is self-sufficient as the nurses know that the women there are cured now. They have birthed and had their confinement. I take Lily back to my bedroom and snuggle her next to me in bed. I have to keep her warm so she will not cry. Her tummy is full, and I am going to try and get one more feed in her, just to top her up. I have smuggled some cow's milk out of the kitchen and stolen two glass feeding bottles from the holding ward. As soon as first light comes, we will be off. I just have to pray to God that Lily will keep quiet as I go out of the main entrance and past the night guard. All I have to do is show him my day pass and we will be safe.

The night drags by, and I do not sleep a wink. I am far too keyed up to sleep anyway. At first light I top Lily up with a small amount of milk, having warmed it against my body overnight. I place Lily into my one and only bag, which is made of a canvas-type material. I used the excuse that I was going to have tea with my aunt and that she would have a new dress for me to wear and more than likely a few reading books, which was why I needed a bag of that size. Hairy Mole was far too bitter with jealousy to even bother to question it. "All right for some, having time off. You don't know you're born, you youngsters," was her only response. Thank goodness. It feels good to get one over on the old cow. Well, hopefully, if my plan works. I still have no idea where Esme is, which is playing on my mind all the time. But for now, I need to concentrate on fulfilling my promise to Esme, keep her baby safe, and find this woman in the woods.

As I pass out of the asylum with no problem, I am struck by the freedom I have. The birds are singing their morning chorus, a beautiful sound. I hear my mother's voice saying to me, "The morning chorus, May. Nature's alarm clock." I am hit again by how much my heart aches for her and my family. I breathe in a big lungful of the early morning air. Wonderful, so utterly wonderful, this smell. The freshness of the spring morning with the faint hue of the honeysuckle and the dampness of the dew on the grass smell like I am experiencing it for the very first time. Once I am well out of sight from the asylum, I open my bag slightly to make sure Lily has some air. I know roughly where I am heading and, in theory, it should not take me long. From previous conversations that I had with Esme, I know I have to find the part of the river that will then lead me to Leonora. I am to look out for an old stone block with the wording "Oxford three miles" engraved into it.

Finally, after I have been walking for what seems like hours, I come across a small clearing which leads down to a sandy bank and the shallow part of the river. Once I find the old stone, I relax. I have reached this part at least. I sit down, my feet and back glad of the rest. Lily is starting to stir, so I give her a few guzzles on her bottle, not daring to let her have too much for fear it will take me longer than I anticipated to find the cottage in the woods. The sun is warming my face as I lift it up to the morning sunshine. It is now 10am. A rabbit runs out in front of me, and I nearly jump out of my skin as I think I have been found out. All my senses are on high alert as I react to every rustle in the trees behind me. It is just a fox or a deer, I suspect, but once the seed of being discovered has been planted in my brain, every little noise has me jumping.

I stay for about half an hour in this spot, slowly acclimatising to the surroundings. I start to think of Esme and how not even a year ago she would sit in this exact spot with Percy, the young man she had given herself to willingly, thinking he would be her one and only. Laughing together, paddling together, talking about their future together before the act of taking her innocence and planting his seed in her. How happy Esme must have felt at that time, those few precious weeks. Then how the horror and total devastation of how he had betrayed her in the cruellest and most heartless way. Finding out he had pledged his love to another, promised this kitchen maid all that he had promised her. The shame that she felt knowing she had let him sully her body, use her, then chuck her away like a piece of rag he used to groom the master's horses. No wonder the poor girl went mad. Esme would have been beside herself, not knowing what to do. She knew nothing of what a man and woman did to make a baby; it would have been totally heartbreaking for her. Then as I sit and think, I imagine the pure, solitary desperation that Esme would have felt. To have no one in the world to confide in. The only way out was to end her misery with death, the dark water beckoning her, enticing her to enter the deep muddy part so she would wade deeper and deeper into the dark abyss and her suffering would soon be over.

I have to get moving again now and find Leonora. The final part of my pact with Esme will be done. I look towards the stone marker and slightly to the left where I should find a very small and narrow clearing through the wood. I am to keep to this path for half a mile then look again to my left, whereupon I should see yet another clearing. I am then to just enter the clearing and look directly to my right, where I should see a tall chimney just clearing the tops of the smaller fir trees.

I do not have long, and I am aware of the time. I have already pinned the note that Esme had told me to write onto Lily's little top. I read the note one more time, tears forming in my eyes as the words blur into one.

Dear Leonora,

Please look after my Lily for me. If you cannot manage her, then please do not take her to the workhouse or to the nuns. My mother might help, but I am very doubtful. I shall come back for my baby as soon as I can. Kiss her and love her and, more than anything else, treat her kindly. I know you will. Tell her I love her. Goodbye for now, my little Lily of the valley.

I cannot stop the tears now as they trickle down my cheeks, my nose running. I knock on Leonora's door with four loud raps. As I am waiting, I notice all sorts of things hanging from the tiny porch. I glance closer to find two bunches of dried lavender and alongside this are some fir cones and a transparent glass ball hanging just below the door. It looks like it contains a few feathers and flowers. The door opens and standing right in front of me is Leonora, looking much younger than I imagined. A small lady but well fed, deep brown hair with flecks of silver beginning to show, kind brown eyes that crinkle at the corners as she smiles. "Hello." I do not know where to start and try my best to explain everything to her. Leonora remembers Esme well, thank goodness. She is telling me what a dreadful state poor Esme was in that awful night.

"If I had been five minutes later coming back from the market, I am afraid things would have ended very differently." I tell her how grateful I am to her for helping Esme that night and go on to explain everything that has happened since then.

"Please will you help, Leonora?"

I am being told to sit and offered a cup of tea and a piece of cake. Whilst I am waiting, I take a chance to look around this ramshackle cottage. Picking Lily up, I rock her in my arms, taking a slow walk around the front room. There is a small fire glowing in the grate surrounded by a well-kept black hearth and matching coal scuttle. A worn rug lays just in front of the fire, and I notice black holes scattered over it where Leonora has not been quick enough to put the fire guard up. Logs are stacked in a neat pile on the right-hand side of the hearth. The two cats are sprawled the full length of the rug, cleaning themselves for a moment before stretching out again and enjoying the warmth of the low fire. A mirror hangs just above a two-seater sofa, which I see is covered in a homemade shawl. A curtain hangs just behind the settee. I try to peek, but it's dark in here, making it difficult.

Just as I go back to sit in a winged-back chair that is covered in a dusky rose velvet material, Leonora enters with a fine-looking teapot. It is pale blue with tiny dark blue forget-me-nots imprinted all over the pot. The teacups are made of China but not a fine bone China like Doctor Jones', though very delicate and pretty all the same. They are a creamy white colour with tiny roses around one side of the cup. A tray of cake is then brought through on the same tarnished silver tray as the tea was delivered. The cake is delicious, and I could eat the whole plateful. There is lemon cake, Victoria jam sandwich cake, and the tastiest coconut sponge with raspberry jam smothered thickly all over the top then just a scattering of shredded coconut. I pour myself a cup of tea as Leonora offers me another piece of cake, my mouth watering at the thought of the lemon sponge. "Well, if you are sure, I would love another piece, please."

Leonora smiles eagerly, looking pleased that I love her cakes so much. "They do not treat you well at the asylum, do they, dear?" she asks knowingly. My mouth is so full of delicious cake that I cannot answer, so instead I manage to shake my head from side to side as I close my eyes and wipe the crumbs from my lips.

After I have drained my hot, sweet dark brown tea, I thank this kind lady, adding, "I haven't tasted tea like that in a very long time."

Lily is starting to stir now, so I lift her up from the soft rug that is just by my chair. I give her some more of her milk and put her against my shoulder, tapping her back gently. "You love her very much, don't you?"

I think for a moment and say, "Yes, I do, very much so."

Next, we head into the cosy kitchen, which is small and very well kept. A fire is heating the black range, a black kettle keeping warm on top of the stove. A Welsh dresser is against the far wall, just behind the square kitchen table, which has a freshly made cob loaf upon it, cooling on a rack. A noise distracts me and as I seek the source of where it is coming from, I see a black bird in a wire cage sat in the small kitchen window. Seeing me looking over, Leonora explains that she had rescued this raven when it was a fledgling as it had a broken wing. As I look closer, I can still see its left wing bandaged to its body.

"It will be ready for release soon enough," the old lady says knowingly.

Under the table, asleep in a basket, is a terrier-type dog, whom the lady informs me is a good little rabbit catcher and keeps her and the cats well fed. It seems to me that Leonora is self-sufficient and lives off the land. She goes on to tell me that she grows her own vegetables and always has a good crop, and how it is more than enough for herself, so she goes to the local market once or twice a week to sell some of her produce.

"My pony and trap serve me well and if it were not for her, I would be stuck."

Leonora makes enough for her and her animals and calls at the grocer on her way back for flour, fat, and sugar to make her cakes.

"What abouts eggs? You would need eggs to make such wonderful cakes."

Leonora also keeps chickens. This lady is a marvel.

Picking up Lily and rocking her gently in my arms, I decide to ask the ultimate question, the question that will make or break the innocent, unknowing Lily's life.

"So, Miss Loney, do you think you can possibly find it within your heart and soul to take this mite?"

Leonora takes the baby from me and looks deeply into her half-closed eyes. "How could I not, May? She has already been through so much. I promise I will take good care of her until the day comes when Esme is well enough to care for Lily herself. Do not fret anymore, May."

My body sags in relief, part of me feeling very guilty over thrusting this baby upon her.

"Don't you worry," Leonora says thoughtfully as if reading my mind. "I have more than enough room and love for this little one." Leonora explains that she has two small bedrooms. One is behind a curtain in the kitchen which has a ladder leading up to it. "I can soon sort that out. It has my lotions and potions in, and I can easily find room elsewhere for them." The other bedroom, which she tells me would be Lily's, is behind another curtain in the front room. She adds, "You know that curtain you were trying to peek into." Leonora had noticed me looking and I feel my face flush with embarrassment. Miss Loney would give old Beady Eye a run for her money, that is for sure. I need not have worried though, as dear Leonora winks and laughs after she has said it. "No, you have nothing to worry about at all." She reassures me again, looking lovingly down at Lily. "We will be fine. I will care for her as if she were my very own. If she gets sick, I will nurse her back to health, as there's not much that nature cannot heal."

I turn away and look out of the window before the tears start again. "My mother always said that," I tell Leonora.

"Your mother was a wise woman then, who I know must of loved you very much." I turn and smile, walk across the room, and hug her. Oh, how I wish in this moment I could stay here too. I have to go back to the doom and gloom of the asylum and try and find Esme.

I kiss the top of Lily's head, but I cannot bear to say the word "goodbye". "Look after our sweet little Lily of the valley." I turn once more as I leave Leonora and her quaint little croft. Wiping away a single tear, I go on my way.

"Three, two, one. You are coming back now, May, to the present day. It is 1996 and all is well. You are fully aware of your surroundings."

My eyes slowly opened as I caught a glimpse of the gold letter opener being put away back in its case. "Where is Esme? Will I ever see her again?" I hardly dared ask Mark, but of course he could not tell me.

Chapter 26

1996

"My feet are killing me. Give them a rub for me, please," I pleaded with Mark. He didn't oblige and I can't say I blamed him. One of the occupational hazards of being a care assistant is having the most fowl-smelling feet. No matter how much I washed them or however much deodoriser I sprayed onto them, they still reeked. Us carers went through no end of shoes. I had experienced a very gruelling shift at St Joseph's on this day and I wasn't sorry to finally be at home with my family.

One of our female patients on the secure ward had somehow managed to escape with a visiting family. This lady, with the name of Edith, looked the picture of innocence, a typical harmless old lady. What you saw and what you got with Edith, though, were totally different. She was a sly, canny old thing and was in the secure unit after she was sectioned. Edith had a criminal record as long as your arm, mainly shoplifting, and as she was a repeat offender, she finally got a prison sentence. Edith hadn't been in prison many months when she started to display some odd and concerning behaviour. Edith started at first to try and take things from the dining area in the prison, just silly things like knives and forks all bundled up together in a paper serviette. This naturally was a cause of concern for the staff, a prisoner with what could be perceived as a weapon. Edith gradually took her strange behaviour up a notch when she started to save her faeces in toilet paper and hide it in her cell. It was not long before the staff could smell the most awful pong and followed their noses. They sent for the prison doctor, who in turn sent for a psychiatrist, both agreeing that it was an obsessive illness that Edith had, her symptoms not dissimilar to collectomania. They also decided that Edith had the start of dementia, hence how she ended up at St Joseph's.

Edith would walk around the unit continuously all day and never seemed to tire herself out. On this day Edith took it upon herself to walk that little bit further, to the nearest town. It was a dreadfully muggy, sultry day, and town was about two miles away. We quickly realised that Edith was missing as we always did half-hourly checks and as soon as we noticed, we activated the missing patient plan. First in the plan was do not panic and check all the rooms and toilets, even places you might think they would never go. Plan two was to send two staff out into the garden. Now I had never experienced plan of action three, until today. Plan three was to call 999 and notify their next of kin. To say it was a frantic, stressful time did not even come close. The police arrived promptly and took two members of staff in the police car to see if they could spot Edith.

After what must have only been a little over half an hour, but seemed more like three hours, we received a telephone call from a local shop, asking us, "Are you missing a patient?" They gave us a very thorough description of a little old lady with white curly permed hair wearing a white blouse with a pale blue cardigan and navy-blue skirt.

"Yes, that's our lady," we heard the matron say before turning to the rest of us and giving a thumbs-up sign. After a brief conversation with the shop owner, it transpired that a young couple had dropped her off in a red car and helped her into the shop. We knew at once who this couple were as they had been the only visitors in that day, visiting the young man's father. Matron first rang the police to explain before sending a familiar face to go and retrieve Edith, far better that than risk Edith having an episode if the police tried to bring her back.

Edith had thoroughly enjoyed her little outing, telling us that she had drunk a lovely cup of coffee, adding, "Better than the muck you pour us in here. Even had a KitKat." She winked.

Matron had telephone the young couple who had inadvertently smuggled Edith out. They were as surprised as anything when Matron told them she was in fact a patient. They went on to explain that they had asked Edith if she liked living here at St Joseph's, to which Edith had replied, "Oh, I do not live here. I am just visiting my husband. Could you give me a lift into town, please? Save me getting a taxi?" So of course they had gladly taken her. How easy Edith must have thought this great escape was. Later during the handover to the next shift coming on duty, we all had a jolly good laugh about it. Naturally this had upturned the whole day, and all our other jobs still had to be completed.

I trudged up the stairs to have a well-deserved soak in the bath. "We can have a takeaway tonight, kiddos," I said on my way up. No chance was I cooking tonight. As I lay in the bath, thinking about the day's adventure, it struck me how different things would have been had this happened one hundred and fifty years ago in the asylum. The patient, after being brought back from escaping, would have been punished in the most barbaric, inhumane way possible, cold-water shock treatment and being left to freeze for goodness knows how long. And that was just for starters. They would have been locked away in the cells until the authorities decided they had learnt their lesson, which could have been days, weeks, or even months. It all depended on who the superintendent in charge was and which way the wind was blowing.

I had been back a couple of times to Mark, who had regressed me back in time, yet I had never once seen Esme. I would search through the miles of corridors, shouting her name repeatedly, all to no avail. I was always met with doors slamming in my face, the empty eyes of faceless attendants who would seem to stare at me, their mouths opening and closing as if they were talking to me, but I could not see them properly. The corridors were blacker than ever. I would put my hands out in front of me as if feeling my way, going around and around in circles. I could touch people and feel the coldness and wetness of their skin, feel the clothes that they were wearing and know the difference between patients and attendants just through the feel of them. Mark explained I could not see Esme or anybody clearly as I was trying too hard to connect with her. I was not fully under regression, and it was more wishful thinking that I would see her again and find out all that had happened to her. I was to leave it a few months and then we could try again.

"Mum. The pizza is here. Come on, we are starving."

I was brought out of my dream world and quickly got out the tub, flinging on my fluffy dressing gown.

"We got French fries as well, Mum," they both echoed. My heart warmed as I looked at them getting so excited over a pizza as we did not have much in our lives, but what we did have was oodles and oodles of love and contentment.

Steve was busy getting the plates out of the cupboard when I yelled, "Forget the plates, Steve. We can eat it out the boxes in the living room. Corrie's about to start."

Steve grinned and said, "You little devil, you."

I laughed and said, "I know, I'm pushing the boat out tonight."

I was watching Toby and Millie tucking into their pizzas and smiling to myself as the grease from the pepperoni and mozzarella was oozing down their chins. Engrossed in every tasty morsel. I took a big swig of my glass of wine and thought how we all deserved a couple of days away at the seaside. I would look tomorrow and see if I could book a caravan somewhere for the summer.

I was off for two days now and I was so looking forward to it. I could take my two to school, which I did miss dreadfully. I missed chatting to the other mums, even Lucinda sometimes. After my two days off, I was to go back to the main ward within St Joseph's as we had to rotate on a two-monthly basis. I was looking forward to seeing Ember again.

I was off to the bingo later the next night to meet up with Sandra and Maggie and there was talk of Colin coming along too. I missed my factory girls, but not enough to ever want to go back. I loved my job caring even though some days were a tough, hard slog. I shall never forget my days at the biscuit factory as I would never have gone on that night out and seen the gimmicky hypnotist. I still cannot stomach a custard cream or chocolate bourbon yet though.

The summer holidays were soon upon us, and we had enjoyed four nights away in a caravan by the seaside. The weather was kind to us for once as normally we were not blessed in that department. Millie and Toby had a wonderful time, eating lots of ice cream and chips, going crabbing and making sandcastles, and at night we would visit the arcades and play the two-penny machines. The concentration was sketched on both their faces as they tried desperately to win a keyring or a packet of sweets. Walking home along the beach, we would look at all the pretty different coloured lights going along the sea front, all wrapped up in our cardies as the chill of the sea air would feel cold against our slightly sunburned skin. All too soon it was time to load the car back up with our belongings, including the cuddly teddy bears or giraffes that they had won at the fair.

Two months later, 1996

I was back on the secure unit at St Joseph's and nothing much had changed apart from a new procedure that had been put in place after Edith's great escape. Any visitors had to come and find a staff member to let them know that they were leaving and there was a book for them to sign upon entering and exiting the ward. We never did get to the bottom of how all three of them managed to get through two supposedly locked doors. I guess human error, and nothing was ever foolproof, especially when Edith was involved.

One gentleman who was called Wilfred was a dear old chap. We would call him Wilf for short and he loved it. Wilf was transferred to us from the main ward as he had become very unpredictable and would often shout out for his mother repeatedly. He had in the past had a total mental breakdown after the death of his mother and then his wife leaving him for another man. He was also one of the last remaining patients that had moved over from the asylum, although by then it was known as a mental health unit. He had also developed the Largactil shuffle through years of being on Largactil and a cocktail of other antipsychotics. This made Wilf extremely unsteady on his feet, resulting in frequent falls. It was after one of these falls that Wilf had fractured his femur and was taken into hospital to have his hip repaired. Wilf was well into his nineties, so the operation was risky.

Wilf made it through the operation and initially was thought to be doing well. One morning, some two weeks after his operation, Wilf developed a nasty chest infection which quickly turned to pneumonia. Unfortunately, none of the antibiotics worked. Wilf was brought back to us at St Joseph's where he was on palliative care, his life nearing the end. We made him as comfortable as we could and placed him on a special mattress that would constantly ripple ever so slightly to help prevent bed sores. We took it in turns to sit with Wilf as he had no known family. We held his hand, stroked his forehead, or read to him. A picture of his beloved mother was placed beside him. Not long after Wilf came back to us, he took a turn for the worst and within days the familiar sound of Cheyne-Stoking had set about him. His mouth was dry, and his lips were cracking. We used a glyceryl lemon-flavoured mouth swab to gently keep his mouth comfortable. Then early one morning, just as Sally and I were changing his pad, Wilf opened his eyes and said, "Mother." He was looking into space with his eyes wide open. I thought for a few precious moments that Wilf was recovering as his eyes had not been open for many days. Sally explained that what we were seeing was known as "the surge". And it is not uncommon for very ill dying patients to have the appearance that they are on the mend and have rallied round. After the surge, death is usually not far behind.

Not long after, Wilf's breathing was getting slower and slower. It was sometimes a minute before he would take another breath. Sally whispered softly in Wilf's ear, "Now you go, Wilf. Go to your dear mother. She is here waiting for you."

Still stroking his head and with me holding his hand, Wilf took his last breath, and all his pain and suffering was over. He was now reunited with his dear mother.

The very last act a nurse or carer can do for their patient is called the last offices, the final act of care. Sally showed me what to do as we gave dear old Wilf his final wash. Sally explained that she always liked to talk to her patients after they had passed over, as she felt it respectful to do so. We would wash Wilf, change his pyjamas, and put a fresh incontinence pad on him. All this time Sally would be saying things like, "OK, Wilf, we are just going to give your face a wash" or "We are just going to be rolling you over onto your side." Sally was an excellent carer and a fantastic, kind, and friendly teacher to me, deeply knowledgeable. There was not much Sally had not seen, and she was unflappable. Once we had washed and changed Wilf, Sally put his false teeth in and combed his hair, shutting his eyes gently with her hand. She asked me to open the curtain slightly and to make sure that the window was ajar. "This will let his spirit out and make his final journey easier."

I loved Sally. She thought of absolutely everything and always put the patients first. I wish that all carers were like Sally, with her genuine kindness and passion. She had forewarned me when we were about to wash and change Wilf for the very last time that I was not to be alarmed that if when we turned Wilf, he sighed or groaned or even tried to sit up. This was all perfectly normal, and it was just the last bits of air leaving Wilf's body. I was so pleased that Sally told me this, as for a first-time carer's experience of performing last offices, this could have been very startling. I thanked Sally and she smiled. "I wish someone had told me about it as I very nearly died myself when I thought that poor old Mavis was coming back from the dead." We both shared a laugh at this sad time, as with this type of work a good sense of humour was a must. How I am so pleased that things have moved on since those awful days in the old Victorian lunatic asylums. I shudder at the sheer thought and memory of it.

One Monday morning at around 10am, I noticed a familiar face walking down the corridor. "Hi, Nancy. How are you?" I enquired.

Nancy looked pale and very drawn, as if she had the weight of the world on her shoulders. "Hello, May. Still struggling with Mother, I am afraid."

Over time Vera had eventually allowed her daughter Nancy to visit. It was a very strained relationship and often Nancy would sit in silence with her mother not knowing what to say to her. Try as she might to engage in some sort of conversation, all Nancy ever got back was a grunt if she was lucky. "I've brought in some old photographs from home to see if that will encourage her to start talking to me."

"Well, it can't hurt," I replied, wishing that I could offer more help. I would make a tray of tea for them both and see if I could prompt some sort of conversation, or at least help them to have a bit of common ground. I set the tray down on the small coffee table by the side of Vera. Deciding to take the bull by the horns, so to speak, I leant over Nancy's shoulder and started looking at some of the photos.

"I love these old photographs. Don't you, Vera?" I gingerly asked.

Vera looked at me from the top of her glasses as if I were mad.

"Who have we here then?" I pointed to an incredibly old sepia photo. Vera had reached over to her side table and got out her magnifying glass, bringing it in and out between the photo and her one open eye. I turned and looked at Nancy, putting my thumbs up.

"That's my old mother. She was a hard bitch," Vera spat venomously. Leaning over, I looked at the faded photo and could just about make out ten or so women all dressed the same, all their faces without expression.

"Which one is your mother?" I ventured. Vera grunted but said nothing. I tried again to get at least some result from this grumpy rude woman. "Where was this photograph taken? Do you know, Vera?"

Vera's head shot round as she snapped, "Of course I know. It was taken at the Victorian lunatic asylum, this town's very own asylum."

I was studying Vera's mole again now and my stomach did its normal ice-cold flip. Could this be a coincidence or something much more? I had to know. "Did your mother work at the asylum then, Vera?"

"She gave her heart and soul to that place and was a fine attendant. Broke her heart when she left to get married and fell pregnant with me. It made her very resentful of me."

At last a breakthrough. I had managed to get more than two words out of Vera. I was shaking now as I took the photograph from Vera, along with the magnifying glass. I took a deep breath and closed my eyes, hardly daring to look. There, second from left, was none other than Hairy Mole, staring solemnly back at me. It was her, no doubt about it. I would recognise that mole anywhere! "Tell me about her life. How did she treat you? Was it all bad? Did she have any love in her at all?" I had so many questions that they were all tumbling out at once.

"Not now. I cannot go into all that now. Another time. The less I think of her, the better."

I do not know how I got through the rest of my shift; it did not seem real to me. Was it real? I needed more to go on than an old faded sepia photograph. I did not sleep a wink that night with all sorts of things whirling around in my mind. I went into work yawning my head off the next morning.

"Good night out, was it, May?" Sally asked amusingly. If only she knew. I had to give myself a good shake-up as I was the carer on wound-dressing today.

Finishing my second cup of strong coffee, I began to feel a bit more human. Violet was first on my list and as I stripped off the bandages, I was pleasantly surprised. The dreadful leg ulcer that Violet had developed some months prior was looking much improved. I was preparing the purple potassium permanganate, ready to start the cleaning and soaking part of the dressing change. "Right then, Violet. If you can put your leg in this bowl for me, please, I will give it a wash and a good soak." Violet always obliged and was never any trouble at all, such a sweet, inoffensive lady.

To kill a bit of time while her leg was soaking, I was admiring all of Violet's trinkets that were dotted about the room. There seemed to be something new each time I went in there. More crystals had appeared and a small bunch of what looked like dried herbs. Violet saw me looking at it and said, "Sage, dear. That is called sage. You burn it and swish it around all the corners of your home to clean the area and banish any bad energy or spirits."

Violet might have been one hundred and one, but she certainly had all her faculties about her. Violet knew the name of every crystal I picked up and could tell me about all its healing properties. "That's amazing, Violet, I never realised crystals could have such an effect on your health and wellbeing."

Violet, looking thoughtful for a moment, added, "There is a cure for anything in nature. If you know what you are looking for."

I was struck dumb for a second. "What did you just say, Violet?" I had to ask again to make sure I had heard right.

"There is a cure for just about anything in nature, dear," Violet repeated to me again.

"I have heard that as well, Violet, many years ago."

Nodding her head knowingly, Violet said, "Yes, my granny taught me all about the old ways and about country living, what you could eat in the hedgerows and what you could not, what were edible mushrooms and what could be deadly if you ingested them." What a wise woman Violet's granny must have been. Violet, as if reading my mind, said, "Well, she was not really my granny, but that is what I always called her. She had taken my mother in as a baby, only days old. My mother would tell me all about her happy childhood growing up in the little cottage in the middle of nowhere. Playing with the animals and going to market with Granny. She had a happy time there."

I sat down on the bed and asked Violet if she had any photographs of her mother and granny. "I have some somewhere. I will ask my old home to help bring them in."

I took a deep breath and asked, "What was your mother's name, Violet?"

She turned her head and, with that sweet smile of hers, replied, "Lily. Mother's name was Lily. Granny and I always called her our little Lily of the valley."

I had to sit back down on the bed and hold it with both of my hands. "Was your granny not your mother's mum then?"

Shaking her head, Violet said, "No. She did come back and contact us, but I was young. Mother spoke of her often and they stayed connected for a while. You know what it is like when you are a child. You never pay much attention to that sort of thing."

My heart was hammering now against my ribs. I just had to ask, "What was your real granny called? Do you have any more information about what became of her?"

Shaking her head again, Violet said, "Yes, I know her name. I shall never forget it as I thought it was such a pretty name. Her name was Esme. Why, dear?"

That had confirmed it for me now. I had come full circle and found out so much. I needed to find out more though. Where did Esme go? Did she have any sort of life? Did she marry and have more children? I needed to know what became of Hairy Mole. I knew she had married and resented her daughter and own husband, but what had caused her to lead such a hateful life, enjoying the cruelty she inflicted on others? And what happened to Beady Eye? Did she have the same fate as Hairy Mole and had to leave the asylum upon marrying?

At last, I had something to go on and I was more determined than ever to find out why Esme seemed to disappear after the birth of Lily. Was it me looking for her too hard, like Mark had suggested? Or was it that she did not want to be found?

THE END

www.ingramcontent.com/pod-product-compliance
Ingram Content Group UK Ltd.
Pitfield, Milton Keynes, MK11 3LW, UK
UKHW042212281224
453045UK00001B/29